UNFRIEND ME

By

TOSHA COSTELLO

No part of this document may be reproduced or
transmitted in any form or by means, electronic,
mechanical, photocopying, recording, or otherwise,
without written permission from the author.

ISBN: 978-0-9995471-2-0

Acknowledgment

To my readers, thank you for your support. I am
humbled, and I am forever grateful.

Disclaimer

TABLE OF CONTENT

Sometimes

it's not the dead we should be afraid of,

but the ones we call friends.

CHAPTER ONE

Everything was quiet as Sarah Woolrich came home from school. "Mom," she called out with joy.

"In the kitchen," Sarah's mom Peggy called out as she took the cookies out of the oven and placed them on the cooling rack. She enjoyed baking. She would often send baked goods to the church and to other organizations. "Well, someone is in a chipper mood today," she said as Sarah walked into the kitchen.

"Mom guess what?" she said with excitement. "I got invited to a party tonight."

"Oh really? And by whom was this invite from?" she questioned.

"Grayson Bradley and his friends. You know the cool kids," Sarah said as she grabbed a bottle of water from the fridge.

"Sarah," Peggy said as she put the last batch of cookies in the oven. "You know how I feel about those kids. They are nothing, but a bunch of bullies that are always up to no good. They are not your friends Sarah," she stated.

All Peggy could think about were the times Sarah came home from school crying from being bullied. The girls would tease her about how she dressed and spread rumors about her just to make themselves look good. She didn't bother to go to the prom, too scared of what could happen. The guys pretended to like her just so that she could do their homework. She was a good kid with excellent grades and kept to herself most of the time.

"Mom please, they want to be my friends now. That's all that matters. If things don't work out I will unfriend them. Plus, this might be my only chance to be cool," she begged.

"What about your friend Jenna? Is she going?"

Jenna was Sarah's best friend. She often got bullied at school too, but not as much as Sarah. Sarah was her own person, but sometimes she felt left out. She often wore her hair black and dressed in dark colors.

"I don't know, but I promise I won't ask to use your car again," she said as she smiled. "And I promise to do all the chores."

"I don't know Sarah. These kids are not your friend. Who else will be there?"

"I don't know. Grayson's friends Becca, Jeffery, Meghan, Alaina and Todd. The cool kids. Mom please," Sarah begged, giving her mom her famous puppy eyes.

After taking a deep breath Peggy gave in. "Ok you can go, but only if there will be grownups there to supervise."

"There will be," Sarah said as she jumped up and down with excitement while she hugged her mom. "I have to go get ready," she said anxiously.

"I honestly don't understand teens being obsessed with being cool and popular."

"I love you too mom," Sarah said as she left to get ready.

Three hours later she came downstairs, ready to leave. "Bye mom!" she yells as she leaves out the door. She disregarded hearing her mom telling her to be home by eleven.

Peggy watched from the window as her

daughter got into a car with her so called new friends. She had a bad feeling about letting Sarah go, but seeing how happy she was, she didn't want to say no.

She counted down the hours as she waited on the living room sofa for Sarah to return home, until she eventually fell asleep.

As she fell asleep, she began dreaming of her daughter. She dreamt that she was on top of a mountain and Sarah was dangling from the edge. She grabbed her hand to pull her up, but she was slipping from her grasp. She could hear her daughter scream over and over, "Mom please help me" as she cried. Before she knew it, Sarah slipped from her hands, causing her to wake up from her dream.

Peggy woke up in sweat, it felt so real. She looked around at the clock on the wall and realized that there was no Sarah. It was way after eleven. She should have been home by now. She tried to call her cell but there was no answer. Each time she would call, her phone would go straight to voicemail. Suddenly her phone rung. It was Sarah.

"Sarah thank God you're alright," she began to say, but she became silent when she heard someone screaming help me, over and over. She knew that voice all too well. A tear slid down her cheek, followed by many more. This wasn't a dream. This was that same feeling that she had when Sarah left. A feeling that will forever haunt her. She knew her Sarah was gone forever but could only hope and prayed that one day she would return.

CHAPTER TWO

ONE YEAR LATER.

The morning was foggy as the dew fell. Claire and her daughter Jess drove in silence. The engine roaring while an eighty's rock band played on the radio.

"Welcome to my hometown sweetie," Claire said out loud cheerfully as her daughter awoke from her sleep. She was from a small town in Connecticut called Wethersfield. She grew up there, but later moved away and was happy to be back. "I think you will love it here Jess. It's where I grew up," Claire said as she took a sip of her coffee. "I stopped and got coffee while you were asleep."

Jess sat in silence. Ignoring her mom wasn't anything new.

"I got you a little gift too," Claire said as she handed her daughter a tiny black box inside of a gift bag.

Jess takes the box and throws it in her purse. She didn't bother to look at it. "I don't want to be here. Why did I have to leave?" Jess whined.

"I told you, your father and I are getting a divorce. He will be working long hours at the firm. We decided it's best for you to stay with me."

"I'm seventeen, I'm old enough to make my own decisions."

"You'll be old enough when you graduate from school and get a job," Claire said as she drove. "Hopefully you'll make better friends."

"There's nothing wrong with my friends," Jess said as she closed her eyes and laid her head against the head rest.

"There's nothing wrong with your friends? Seriously Jess? For Christ sake look at you. You're dressing like a whore, curse like a sailor and your grades are failing. You've gotten out of control Jess. I don't even know if you are still a virgin." She turns the radio down and glanced over at her daughter and waited for a reply.

Jess turns the radio back on. This time louder than before and started singing along with the rock music playing.

"Jess, are you still a virgin?" she said over the loud music.

"Seriously mom? Why are you even asking me this?" She turns and stares out the window. The fog made it hard to see the trees. Only the streetlights were still visible.

"Because," Claire turns the radio off. "You're my daughter, I have the right to ask. Plus, I don't want to be going around saying that you are if you're not," Claire stated as she takes another sip from her coffee.

"Oh, my goodness mom! Why are you even going around telling people anyway!? You are seriously trying to ruin my life!" Jess shouted as she turns the radio back up and continued staring out the window.

"Jess!" Claire yelled as she turned the radio off.

"Mom!" Jess yelled back turning the radio as loud as it would go.

Claire knew her daughter was a spoiled brat. She was the only child and always got whatever she wanted, mostly from her dad, but right now Claire has had enough. She reaches over to turn the radio off, right as Jess tries to block her, causing her to spill hot coffee over her leg and the seat. "Dammit Jess!" she yells as she immediately grabs a napkin from the cup holder and begins wiping her leg.

"I'm sorry mom. I didn't mean to," Jess said sympathetically.

"Just hand me those other napkins out of there," she said as she pointed towards the glove compartment. She then continued wiping up the mess that was made, while trying to watch the road. "I don't know what has gotten into you lately."

Jess reaches down and retrieves the other napkins." Mom watch out!" she yells as her mom looks up.

Claire suddenly slams on the breaks, causing the car to slide against the damp road. She loses control as the car veers off onto the side of the road. The car tires skid against the gravel, kicking up small pebbles as it comes to a halt. They were both breathing hard as their hearts pounded against their chest.

"Are you ok?" Claire asked.

"Yeah." Jess said as she nodded.

"She just came out of nowhere," Claire said as she hurried to unbuckle her seatbelt and unlock her door.

"Mom, what are you doing!?" She quickly grabs her mom's arm.

"What do you think I'm doing? I'm going to make sure she's ok," Claire said as she opens her car door and got out. "Hello?" she calls out as she looks for the girl.

Jess stayed inside as she was told. Her eyes wide with fear as she scanned the outside looking for any sign of the bystander. She rolls the driver side window down and yells out, "Mom let's go, she's gone already!" Something didn't feel right. She felt like someone was watching her. An uncanny feeling cradles her body, causing chills to travel down her spin as she continues to look around. "Oh my gosh!" she gasps as she discovers a handprint on her window. Hesitantly, she takes her left hand and places it on the window, carefully matching it against the handprint. She belts out a loud wrenching scream.

"Jess!"

"Mom!" Jess yells as she sobbed while holding her hand.

Claire hurried back to the car and finds Jess holding her blood dripping hand. "Jess! What did you do? What happened to your hand?" Claire asked frantically as she got in and closed the door.

"I didn't do anything," Jess cried.

"What happened!?" her mom questioned.

"I........ I don't know," she stuttered.

"Here, give me your hand." Claire takes her scarf and wraps it around Jess's hand. "We need to get you to a doctor."

"No. I'm ok," she flinched. "It just hurts a little."

"We need to let someone look at it," Claire said as she finished wrapping up Jess's hand.

"No mom, I'm ok."

Claire takes a deep breath. She hated to argue and arguing with Jess always seems like an uphill battle. "Fine, but as soon as we get home we're putting something on it. We don't need it getting infected."

"Whatever, can we just go please?" Jess said as she stared out her window. Uncertain of what just happened and what she just saw.

"We can't just go. I'm waiting on the police to arrive."

"What!? Mom!?' Jess yelled.

"Well I can't just leave. She could be hurt and scared."

"If she was hurt, she would have never run mom."

"You know, I just don't understand how you got like this."

"Got like what?" Jess questioned.

"Heartless. This isn't you."

"You don't know me," Jess replied.

Claire just stared at her daughter. She often wondered, where in life did she go wrong with Jess. No matter how hard she tried, being the perfect mother just wasn't perfect enough.

Claire looked up and saw lights in the rearview mirror. "Finally," she said as she rolled down her window.

The Officer exited his patrol car and made his way towards them. "Morning folks."

"Morning officer," Claire said as she extended her hand. "I'm Claire Vanderbilt and this here is my daughter Jess." She began telling the officer what had happened.

"I'm going to look around to see where she may have possibly gone to. So, if you folks could sit tight, I will be right back," the officer said as he left and headed towards the wooded area, surrounded by tall grass and trees. He returned fifteen minutes later with no findings. "Didn't see anything or anyone," he said.

"Are you sure? I... I mean we both saw her."

"We get a lot of phone calls for runaways. Maybe.... this is the case," he stated.

"Maybe. Is it possible to give me a

call? Just so I will know if she's ok." Claire takes out a small piece of paper and writes her name and number down on it.

The officer stares at it before taking a card out of his shirt pocket and handing it to her. "If you find out anything, call this number on here, my direct number."

"Thank you, officer...?"

"Bradley.... Officer Bradley."

Jess didn't like the way Officer Bradley was looking at her mom. "Mom please.... can we just go?"

"Sorry Officer, it's been a very long morning."

"I understand. Enjoy the rest of your day." He said before getting back in his patrol car and driving off.

Claire looked at her daughter, the silence spoke for itself. She then started the car and drove off as well.

CHAPTER THREE

THREE WEEKS LATER

It was girl's evening out for Claire as she got ready to leave. Jess had her new friends over from school. She quickly made friends on her first day. The same friends that befriended Sarah. They were the popular crew at school. They were bullies at their best. Some of the kids wanted to be them, while the others wanted them dead.

Claire stood in the door way of Jess's room as she slips on her shoes. "Jess, I'm getting ready to leave," she said.

"Ok mom," Jess said as she continued talking with her friends.

"Remember girls, no boys."

"Ms. Vanderbilt, we are never thinking of boys," Alaina said as the others giggled.

"You ladies can't fool me. Remember I've been young before too," Claire said as she sat on the edge of the bed.

"Mom, we're trying to study here."

"Ok, ok, well, I guess I will get going. I will be back before dinner. You have all my numbers saved in your phone, right Jess?"

"Yes mom."

"Ok dear," Claire said as she kissed Jess on top of her head and left.

"Yes we have the house to ourselves!" Meghan yelled.

"Did you see how Grayson looked at you today? I think he really likes you," Alaina said.

"No way. We are just friends," Jess stated.

"We should invite him and his friends over," Meghan suggested.

"No way, my mom would totally flip out."

"Who cares," Becca said. "Did you actually think we were going to study?" Becca said as she stood in front of the mirror and began putting on lip gloss. She often acted as the leader. Whatever she wanted to do, Meghan and Alaina would follow in her footsteps.

"I told my mom we were going to study, so yeah," Jess said.

"How about I go call him now?" Alaina said as she grabbed Jess's phone and ran into the bathroom.

Jess ran behind her, but she wasn't quick enough. "Hey!" she yells. "Alaina! I'm not playing! Don't you dare call him!" she yells again as she bangs on the door.

"Don't worry, mommy won't find out," Meghan laughed.

Jess just looked at Meghan. If looks could kill, she'd be the first to die. She began banging on the door again. "Alaina, open the door. Alaina?" Jess called out.

"Maybe, she's taking a shit?" Becca laughed, but soon stopped when she realized she was the only one laughing. "Alaina open the door," she said as she now began banging on the door as well.

Still no sound from Alaina. All fun and jokes soon began fading away. "Alaina," Jess called out. She was beginning to panic as she placed her ear to the bathroom door.

"Can you hear her?" Meghan asked as she stood there scared. Heart beating faster than a freight train. "This isn't funny Alaina!"

Jess could hear a faint voice cry, "help me." She turned and looked at Meghan and Becca. "You guys hear that?" she asked.

"Hear what?" Meghan asked.

"I hear another voice coming from the bathroom," said Jess.

"This is seriously freaking me out," Becca said as she scanned the bedroom, looking for something to break the door in with. "We need to break the door in!"

"What? Are you crazy? My mom would never let me have friends over again if she comes in and finds the door busted open," Jess said.

"Then what are we supposed to do? Just leave her locked in there?" Becca argued.

"I don't know," Jess replied.

"What if she's dead?" Meghan asked.

"She's not dead!" Jess yells.

"Well, what if something has her?" Becca asked.

"She's not dead and nothing has her. Maybe she's trying to scare up. So guys chill the fuck out before………………"

Before Jess could finish her sentence, a blood screeching scream came from the bathroom.

"Alaina!" Becca yells. "We need to break this door down now!

They were right, she wasn't coming out. Jess's mom would never let her have friends over again, but what was she supposed to do? Friends have each other's backs.

"Ok, on the count of three we break the door down," Jess said as she looked at Becca and Meghan. They didn't say a word, they just shook their head ok. Jess began counting, "one, two…." On the third count the door opens. Jess looks back at her friends.

"I'm not going first. It's your house, you should go first." Becca said.

"We all go together. This wouldn't

have happened if you didn't have to suggest calling Grayson," Jess said.

"Fine we all go," Becca said with an attitude.

They slowly opened the door wider and began walking in. "Gosh what is that smell?" Meghan said with a disgusted face as she covered her nose.

"See, I told you she took a shit," Becca said with a I told you so face.

Jess rolled her eyes and didn't bother to comment. "Alaina?" Jess calls out. She sees her phone laying in the middle of the floor. As she bends down to retrieve it, she noticed movements out of the left corner of her eye.

"Alaina," they all called out in a sigh of relief as they hurried to her. She was hiding under the bathroom vanity, shaking and frightened as if she had seen a ghost.

"Alaina what happened?" Becca questioned as she helped her from under the vanity.

For a minute she didn't say anything. She just stood there staring at Jess.

"What?" Jess questioned.

"What did you do?" Alaina angerly asked.

"I didn't do anything. You took my phone and ran in the bathroom and now I'm at fault?" Jess said.

"I was only joking with you!" Alaina yelled. "You didn't have to turn the light off and lock the door and you guys let her!"

"What? What are you talking about? I didn't touch the light." Jess replied.

"Yeah Alaina, she didn't." Meghan said. "We were all trying to get the door open, before you finally opened the door."

"Wait, wait, wait. I didn't open the door. You saw where I was," Alaina said.

"Yeah, but you could have also opened the door and ran back under the vanity," Jess said.

"I didn't do such thing bitch!" Alaina yelled.

"Hey!" Becca yelled, trying to calm Jess and Alaina before things got out of hand. "Let's just forget that any of this happened.

We're all friend's, right? So, let's act like it," Becca said before grabbing her things. "We're studying downstairs." Then she stormed off.

Everyone grabbed their things and headed downstairs. "This isn't over bitch," Alaina said as she passed by Jess.

"Yeah whatever," Jess said as she closed her bedroom door and followed the others downstairs.

CHAPTER FOUR

The steam from the shower covered the bathroom mirror as Jess reached her arm out and grabbed a towel from the towel bar.

"Jess," a voice softly whispers her name.

"Mom?" Jess calls out as she continued drying off.

"Jess," the voice whispers again.

"Mom that's not funny," she said as the floor squeaked.

The shower curtains began to move, someone was there.

"Mom…. this isn't funny. You're scaring me," her voice cracked as her body was trembling with fear. Once the footsteps subsided, she calmed her nerves and yanked the shower curtains back. No one was there, just the steam and a pungent smell filled the air.

"Gosh what is that smell?" she said as she stepped out of the shower and finished drying off.

As fear still cradles over her body, the cold floor beneath her feet sent chills down her spine as she slowly walks into her bedroom. Looking around, she noticed the window was open. The sheer white curtains danced against the window as the cool air drifted in. She could feel someone watching her.

She walks over to the window and closes it, just as her door opened.

"Jess," her mother called out as she opened the door.

"Mom do you ever knock?"

"I didn't know I had to knock in my own house. Anyway, dinner is ready," Claire said before closing the door.

Jess finished getting ready and headed downstairs for dinner.

"So how was school today?"

"It was ok," said Jess as she played with the food on her plate.

Claire studied Jess, "what's the matter?"

"Who said anything was the matter?"

"I had you remember; a mother knows when something is wrong with her child."

"If I told you, you wouldn't believe me," Jess said as she played with the food on her plate.

"Try me. Give me a chance before you close me off. I'm your mom, whatever it is we can get through it together."

She thought about it and gave in. "Ok...well...I've been having these dreams. They seem so real."

"Honey they are just dreams. Could it be something you watched on tv?" Claire said as she ate her dinner.

"No. They're not. I just know it. Every night in my dreams......... I see this girl," Jess said.

"What girl?" Claire asked curiously as she placed her fork down and stops eating. She knew that she was taking a chance by moving here, but never knew it would come to this. She didn't believe in that paranormal stuff or ghosts. Those things only happen in movies, they don't happen in real life.

"She has this long black hair that partially covers her face. She looks creepy mom. The craziest thing is......I never see her face," Jess said as she looked at her mom.

"Jess sweetie..." Claire was worried about her daughter.

"I'm not crazy mom!" she yelled as she got up from her seat and carried her plate to the kitchen counter.

"I never said you were crazy!" Claire yelled back as she follows her into the kitchen, calming her tone before saying anything else. "Look, I know this transition has been hard on you."

Jess turns around. "I saw her before mom. On the way home. That person that we almost hit, I believe it was her. I didn't see her face, but I know it was the same person. I'm not crazy mom. The kids at school said a girl used to stay here with her mom.?"

"I know dear, but you know that it's not possible."

"I saw a handprint on my window, I

touched it, and something happened. What if she's the girl?"

"That's not possible Jess."

"Why huh? Why can't it be possible. You never believe……"

"Because she's missing!" Claire yelled, cutting her daughter off before she could finish.

"What do you mean she's missing? How do you know this?"

"When I bought the house, the realtor said that something happened to the daughter. She didn't go into details, but she just wanted to let me know. I didn't think anything of it."

"You didn't think to include me in it. This is my life too!" Jess yells as she ran upstairs.

"Dammit," Claire said as she cleared off the table and headed upstairs to her bedroom.

Once upstairs she immediately grabs her laptop and began searching online for information about the previous owner. "Oh, my goodness," she gasps. She grabs for her glasses and continued reading. "Sarah

Woolrich," she whispers. She reached for her cellphone and began dialing. "Frank call me as soon as you get this message. It's important. I can't explain it right now, but I really need for you to call me," she said as she left a message on her ex-husband's voicemail. She then texted him soon after.

A knock came at the door.

"It's open Jess," Claire called out while still staring at the laptop screen. "Jess? It's open," she called out again, this time setting aside her laptop. An eerie feeling gave her chills. Something wasn't right. "Jess?" She eases up from her bed, softly placing her feet on the cold hardwood floor. Just as she got to the door, the door opens and Claire screams.

"Mom!?...."

"Jesus Christ Jess!!" she screamed. You're trying to give me a heart attack?" Claire said as she placed her hand over her chest.

"What are you doing?"

"I thought I heard you at the door," Claire said.

"No, I was downstairs getting something to drink."

"Oh...ok. You're ok?"

"Yeah. I just wanted to know, if I could sleep in here with you tonight?"

"Of course, you can dear," Claire said as she closed her laptop and laid her reading glasses on the nightstand.

Jess climbed into her mom's bed. "Mom, why did you and dad break up?"

This was one conversation Claire knew she wasn't ready to have. At some point she knew she needed to have it.

"Jess maybe this isn't the right time to...."

"Mom...I'm seventeen. I'm not a baby anymore. I can handle whatever it is," Jess said while looking her mom directly in the eyes.

"He found someone else...... that he was happy with," Claire said while trying not to let her eyes fill with tears.

"Why?"

"I don't know. Some people, they fall out of love I guess."

"Do you still love him?"

That was a question she didn't want to answer right now. "Jess why don't we call it a night. Ok?"

"Ok, good night mom."

"Good night Jess," Claire said as she tucked her in.

No matter how tough Jess seemed to act, deep down inside she was a sweet girl and no matter how old Jess gets, she will always be her baby.

CHAPTER FIVE

The room was quiet...a little too quiet. The only thing you could hear was the soft breathing of Jess and Claire as they slept.

The pungent smell returned, while the cool air drifted in, causing the curtains to once again dance against the window.

Jess began to toss and turn. She began to whimper. "No...please.... don't kill me. Please.... please don't kill me," she cried. She became louder and louder, repeating herself over and over, waking up her mom. "Help me, please help me," she cried.

"Jess," Claire said as she tried waking up her daughter, but Jess continued to whimper and cry. She reached over and turned on the table lamp. "Jess wake up sweetie!" she said louder. This time shaking her, hoping to wake her up. "Jess!"

"Mom?" Jess said as she opened her eyes. "I'm here sweetie," Claire said as she held her daughter close.

"Mom," Jess cried.

"Shhhhh, it's ok. It was just a bad dream," Claire whispers as she continued to hold Jess.

"It felt so real mom," said Jess as she continued to sob. Holding her mom as close as she could.

All kinds of things went through Claire's mind. She began to wonder if moving back home was more of a bad idea than good. What has she gotten them into? She questioned herself.

"Mom, it's so cold," said Jess as her body trembled against the cold air.

Claire looks and sees the open window. She hurries to close it and noticed a stench in the air but thought nothing of it. "How did that get opened?" she said out loud as she returned to bed. "Why don't you try to get some sleep."

"I can't. Sometimes it feels like someone is watching me," Jess said.

"No one is watching you. You just had a bad dream. We all have them occasionally."

"Didn't grandma say that, if you dream

of someone dead, it means that they are in the room with you?" Jess said as her body shook.

Nights like this, is the reason why Claire hated when her mom would tell scary bedtime stories to Jess when she was little. "Sweetie your grandma was just making things up. They're not true. You know how she can be."

"But what if it is true? What if she's really dead and she's trying to tell me something?"

Claire didn't know what to say. She held her daughter tight and prayed that her ex-husband Frank would return her call. Sending Jess back was for the best. Just until things were back to normal. As much as she wanted to keep her daughter there with her, she knew that doing so would do more harm than good.

"Honey she's not dead. She probably ran away," said Claire.

"But why? Why am I dreaming of her? Why is she in my dreams? I've never met her before. Never even seen a picture of her."

"I wish I knew the answer, but I don't. Things will get better," said Claire.

For a while they both sat in silence as Claire held her daughter. She really needed answers and needed them right away.

"Jess?"

"Yes mom."

"You know there are good doctors that can also help," Claire said as she felt Jess pull away from her.

"What? You think I'm crazy?" Jess asked as she looked at her mom in disbelief.

"No…no that's not what I'm saying."

"Then what are you suggesting mom, because it sounds like to me you don't believe me, again. You never believe me," Jess said as she began to cry.

Claire grabbed hold of her daughter and held her tight. "I believe you," said Claire.

"No, you don't. You think I'm crazy," Jess said between sniffling.

"Jess sweetie, I don't think you're crazy. Let me go get you some Kleenex," Claire said as she got up and hurried to the bathroom and hurried back.

"Mom."

"Yes sweetie'"

"Can I go stay with dad?" Jess asked as she held her head down. She didn't want to see the disappointment on her mother's face.

"Is that what you truly want?" Claire asked as she took hold of her daughter's hand, while looking directly at her, but her daughter's eyes wouldn't meet her gaze.

"No. It's not what I truly want," said Jess. This time meeting her mother's gaze. "What I truly want is for you and dad to get back together. He still loves you."

"No. No he doesn't," Claire replied as she held her head down.

"Yes, he does. I can tell by the way he still looks at you."

"Jess, he's in love with someone else."

"He doesn't love her. I just know it mom. He wouldn't do this to us. Dad loves you...he loves us."

Claire could hear the hurt in her daughter's voice. Jess tries to play hard and tough, but she was still that sweet optimistic little girl that she once knew.

"So, tell me, what do you know about love?" Claire asked while smiling.

"I know enough mom, I'm not a little girl anymore."

"I know. If you ever have questions about love or anything else, you promise to talk to me?"

"I promise mom."

"And for the record, no matter how old you will get, just know that you will always be my little girl."

"I know mom," Jess said as she laid back in her mom's arms.

Claire held her daughter until she eventually fell asleep. Trying not to wake her, she eases her down, grabs her laptop and begins searching the web for the disappearances of Sarah Woolrich.

"Ok Sarah, what happened to you and

why are you bothering my daughter?" Claire said to herself as she continued searching online.

Twenty minutes had passed and still she couldn't locate any information on Sarah. Everything was the same on every site that she went to. She would have to do her own research, but for now she was calling it a night.

CHAPTER SIX

Claire was awakened by a knock at the door, followed by the doorbell ringing. She looks over at the clock. "What in the world," Claire said. She eases out of bed slowly, trying not to wake Jess who was sleeping peacefully. Whoever it was, was knocking like a crazy person.

"I'm coming, I'm coming hold your horses," Claire said as she rushed down the stairs. "This better be important," she said out loud as she opened the door.

"Good morning Ms. Vanderbilt, I hate to disturb you so early," Officer Bradley said as his eyes roamed over Claire's figure.

"Morning Officer Bradley. May I help you?" she asked.

"I was wondering if I could speak with you briefly about the girl you saw a few weeks ago?"

"Um...yeah sure. Come in please," Claire said as she opened the door. "Can I get you anything to drink?"

"No thank you, I'll only be a minute."

"You can have a seat anywhere. Please excuse the mess, we still have a lot of unpacking to do," Claire said as she had a seat on the couch, while Officer Bradley sat in a chair across from her. "Ok so what's the news? Is she ok?"

Officer Bradley looked at Claire as if he had some terrible news, like whatever he had to say was hard to say.

"Well, tell me she's ok."

Officer Bradley reached inside of his jacket and handed Claire a picture. "Is this the girl you saw?"

Claire takes the picture and carefully examines it. She was young and probably the same age as Jess. "This...this is her," Claire said as she looks up from the picture. "Is she ok?"

"Ms. Vanderbilt…...she disappeared a little over a year ago. Her name is Sarah Woolrich. Claire began thinking about the conversation she and her daughter had. This can't be real. "Ok...well that's a good thing, right? It means that she is alive. She's still out there."

"We all hope so. The case has been closed. No hard evidence was ever found."

"So just like that, the system gives up? This is someone's daughter we're talking about. What if she's out there hurt?" Claire said as she got up and began pacing the floor.

"Also, I don't know if you were informed, but she and her mother stayed in this house."

"Yeah, I was informed of a girl and her mother, but didn't know the names until recently. Actually…...last night. I did a little research of my own," she said as she looked at Officer Bradley. "I would appreciate it if you didn't mention any of this to my daughter. She's already having a tough time adjusting to this move."

Officer Bradley was about to speak when suddenly Jess appears in the background. The stare that she gave him wasn't normal, she didn't seem normal, which startled him.

"Mom," Jess said as she came down

the stairs. "What's going on?"

Claire looked up, "Jess what in the world happened to your hair?" she questioned and then looked over at Officer Bradley. Both wondering how long she had been standing at the top of the stairs. Trying to regain her composure, Claire finally calmed her nerves.

"Jess, you remember Officer Bradley from a few weeks ago. He was just stopping by to see how we were doing," Claire said as she looked over at Officer Bradley again, making sure they were on the same page.

Officer Bradley stood up from his seat. His eyes went directly to Jess. She was wearing something that looked so familiar to him.

"Hi," Jess said as she stared at Officer Bradley.

"Hi, that's a nice necklace you got there."

She looks down at her necklace. "Thanks, mom picked it up for me when we first got in town." Jess looks over at her mom and gave a little smile.

Officer Bradley knew that he had seen that same necklace before, but it would be impossible. There was no way that this was possible. Something just didn't seem right.

"Well, I should get going," Officer Bradley said as he made his way to the door with Claire following behind him.

"Thank you for stopping by Officer Bradley, I really appreciate it. I was about to start making breakfast, you're welcome to join us."

"I really should get going," he said again as he turned around and left.

He looked frightened. Claire stood in the doorway until Officer Bradley was gone. She closed the door and locked it as she rested against it. Her mind flooding with thoughts of "what the fuck did I get us into."

Now to deal with Jess and her hair, she thought as she pushed herself away from off the door. "Jess," Claire calls out.

"In the kitchen mom," Jess replied. She sat at the kitchen counter eating a bowl of cereal.

Claire stood there, just looking at Jess

before walking up to her and running her fingers through her hair.

"Mom what are you doing?" Jess said as she got up from her seat.

"What happen to your hair?"

"What do you mean what happen? I dyed it black."

"But why?"

Jess gave her mom that crazy look. That look that indicates a stupid question. "Because I wanted to. It's my hair."

"You know what, you're right. It's your hair. You can do whatever you like. Dye it pink if it makes you happy."

Jess hugs her mom then kissed her on the cheek. "See, I knew you would understand. Can we go shopping today? I really need new clothes for school."

"Jess you just went shopping. Every time you get money doesn't mean you have to spend it," Claire said as she made herself a cup of coffee. Jess's dad had paid her credit card bill this month. Claire was against her having one, but her husband insisted. He felt that it would teach her financial responsibility. Now Claire mostly pays her bill. She looked at it as an extra cost.

"Mom please, I just need a few things. Plus, I'm supposed to be meeting up with my friends."

"Ok fine, just let me go get ready."

After a few minutes, Claire returned downstairs and they both left.

CHAPTER SEVEN

After three hours of shopping, Claire and Jess returned home.

"Jess grab that bag on your side," Claire said as she retrieved the bags from her side. Something above caught her attention. "Gosh that window is opened again?"

Jess was already at the door unlocking it. Nothing appeared odd or out of place.

"I was surprised to see Officer Bradley there. I can't believe he's Grayson's dad. We should invite them over for dinner one day," Claire said as she kicked her shoes off.

"No thank you, the only thing you are going to do is interrogate him. Plus, we are just friend's mom. I'm going to put my things up," Jess said as she ran upstairs to her room. A few seconds later came a terrifying scream.

"Jess!" Claire calls out as she ran up the stairs and sees her daughter standing in the doorway. "Jess, what's wrong!?"

Jess was too terrified to say anything. She just pointed instead.

Claire pushed the door all the way open and gasped at what she saw. "Oh God," she said as her hands covered her mouth and nose. The smell reeked.

All over the walls were the words "UNFRIEND ME" written in red.

"Oh, my goodness! Jess go get my phone."

"But mom,"

"Just go…now!"

Jess ran downstairs as fast as she could and returned with her mom's phone.

Jess walked into her room and began snapping pictures with her phone, while her mom called 911.

"Jess don't touch anything, we need to leave. We can wait downstairs for the cops," Claire said as she grabbed Jess by the arm. "Who in the hell would do such a thing. Break in and paint such crap on the wall. Fucking assholes." Claire paced the floor, scared, angry and upset.

Jess sat quietly on the couch, scrolling through the pictures that she had just taken of her room. "Mom, I don't think this was random. This house has been vacant for a while before we moved in. Why would someone suddenly vandalize it now?"

Claire stared at Jess. She could care less right about now. She just needed some answers.

Blue lights filled the yard. "Thank God," Claire said as she peeked out the window. "The cops are here." She opened the door just as a knock came. "Officers please come in."

"I'm officer Glenn and this is my partner, Officer Dale. Do you mind showing us where the room is?"

"Sure, it's right this way," Claire said as she led the officers upstairs. "We had just come in from shopping, my daughter came upstairs to her room and suddenly I heard her scream." Claire was rambling, and she knew it, but didn't care. She had something to say and dammit they were going to listen. "I don't know what came over someone to do this to my house."

Officer Glenn opened the door to Jess's bedroom. The stench was so horrific that Officer Glenn had to close the door. "I wasn't prepared for that," he said.

"I'm sorry, I forgot to mention the terrible odor," she said.

He has seen many vandalism cases, but this was of something that he has never seen. He looked at his partner, "you ready?" he asked.

"Ready as ever," Officer Dale replied.

As they braced themselves, they entered the bedroom. "What the hell happened in here?" said Officer Dale. "Smells like someone died."

"Oh gosh." Fear began creeping all over Claire's body.

"Was the window open when you arrived?" Officer Glenn asked.

"Yes, it was the first thing I noticed, but for some reason, I didn't think anything of it."

Both officers just looked at each other. Wondering if they should believe her or not.

"What? What's that look for? You think I'm making this up or something!" Claire yelled, not noticing Jess in the doorway.

"Mom," Jess said.

"This is our life here. We just moved here a few weeks ago. I can't make......."

"Mom!?" Jess yelled, finally getting her mom's attention. "A Detective Armstrong is wanting to speak with you, he's downstairs."

"Ok.... I'll be right there," Claire said as Jess returned downstairs. Claire looked around at the two officers, feeling bad for going off on them. "I'm so sorry, please forgive me. It's just been one thing after another since we've moved in," she said before leaving out of the room.

"Ms. Vanderbilt," Detective Armstrong called out as Claire was coming down the stairs.

"Hi Detective......Daniel?"

"Claire? Claire Vanderbilt? Long time no see."

"You're a Detective now?" Claire asked as she gave Daniel a hug.

"Six years and counting," Detective Armstrong said.

"You two know each other?" Jess asked.

"Of course, we were high school sweethearts," he replied.

"No wonder you wanted to come back," Jess said as she went in the kitchen.

Claire didn't bother to go there with her daughter, at least not right now. They had more important matters to take care of.

"Sorry about that," she said.

"It's ok. I understand," he replied.

"You have teenagers too?" she asked.

"Oh no," Detective Armstrong laughed. "I have a niece and nephew. Their father isn't around, so I try to be there as much as possible. I...um...I haven't found anyone to settle down with since you walked out of my life," he said as he looked Claire directly in her eyes.

She didn't know what to say. She just stood there with her heart racing. Feelings that were stored away came rushing back.

"Well, I'm going to go and look at the room, I'll be back to discuss any findings that we may come across," Detective Armstrong said before heading off in that direction.

Claire didn't say a word, she just shook her head. All these years she never knew Daniel still had feelings for her. She turns around and sees Jess standing in the doorway.

She walks over to the sofa and has a seat. She's back to herself again. The same Jess that ignores her mom and pushes everyone away when she feels like she's being mistreated. She didn't know exactly why her mom and dad were getting a divorce. Claire never went into details. She often thought about telling her, but never knew when the right time was.

"Jess," Claire said.

"No need to explain mom. It's all about you. I don't exist, at least not to you."

"Jess don't say that. You're my only child and you know I love you. I moved us here to start over. I want the best for you and you know this."

"Then why did you leave dad? If you wanted what's best for me, why did you take me from everything that I know?"

Tears began to form in Claire's eyes. Even through all the craziness that's going on, now was the perfect time to let her daughter know. She deserves to know the truth.

"The truth is……"

"Ms. Vanderbilt." Claire looked around to her name being called by Detective Daniel.

"We'll talk later, I promise," Claire said to Jess before turning to Detective Armstrong. "So, what's the verdict?" Claire said nervously.

"Well, even though the window was up when you got home, it doesn't appear to be a break in."

"So, what are you saying?"

"Whoever did this, has been here before. Maybe they used a spare key and left the window up as a distraction. The lock on the window isn't broken. Out of all these windows in this house, they chose that window, but that's not what concerns me."

"I'm afraid to ask?"

"The writing on the wall isn't written in paint, it's written in blood."

"Oh God, are you sure?" she asked.

"Well, I've seen my share of blood and I'm almost certain this is what we have here. We will send it in to the lab for a positive ID."

"So, are we even safe to stay here?" Claire asked.

"As of now yes. The outside has been searched, as well as the inside. A crew is waiting outside to cleanup."

"What about the girl?" Jess asked.

"What girl?" Detective Armstrong asked.

"I overheard mom talking to Officer Bradley. He mentioned that a girl and her mom used to live here. The girl went missing and was never found," Jess said as she looked at her mom.

Claire updated Detective Armstrong

with everything that had happened, starting with the first day they arrived in town, up until now.

"We will get to the bottom of this. It could be some teens playing games, but I promise we will find out."

"Ok," Claire said. He could tell she was still frightened and shaken up. All he wanted to do was hold her.

"If you would like, I can get the guys to do one last walk through?"

"That would be awesome Detective. Thank you."

"Please, just call me Daniel. We've known each other long enough, don't you think?"

"Sorry," she said as she held her head down and smiled.

Daniel walked to the door. "Well, I need to get going. If you need anything please call me," Daniel said as he handed her his card.

"Ok, thanks again." Claire said as she stared at his card.

"Take care," he said before opening the door and leaving.

CHAPTER EIGHT

An hour left before the school day was over. Jess was tired and exhausted from lack of sleep. With every second that passed, it was getting harder and harder to hold her head up. Finally, she gave in and let sleep consume her. Fifteen minutes later the school bell rang, and she hurried outside. "Hey, Jess wait up," a male voice called out.

"Oh, hey Grayson," she said.

Grayson and Jess were good friends.

"Your mom still freaking out about dying your hair black?"

"Not really. I think she finally realizes that I'm not a kid anymore," Jess said as she gave a quick smile.

"What are you doing later?" he asked as he grabs Jess's hand, catching Jess off guard.

She quickly removes her hand. "I'm studying with Becca and Meghan, apparently Alaina is still mad at me," she said as she kept walking.

"Yeah, I heard about what happened, but don't beat yourself up over it. Sooner or later she'll come around. She's a really good person."

"I guess," Jess replied in a dry tone.

"Is something else wrong? Did I do something wrong?" Grayson asked as he blocks her steps, bringing her to a stop.

"I just have a lot to do, that's all. Exams and stuff."

"How about I walk you home?"

"Umm......ok," Jess said as she looks over her shoulder and realized someone was staring at her. "Who is that? She's been staring at me since I started school."

"That weirdo? That's Jenna Davis. She was a friend of the girl that died."

"Who? Sarah Woolrich?"

"Yeah, they were both fucking weirdos."

"I thought she was just missing. Who said she died?" Jess asked.

"Well, it's been almost a year, I'm

assuming she's dead. I never really met her."

They continued walking until they were halfway to Jess's house.

"So, how do you like staying there in the old Woolrich house?

"Ok I guess. Well thanks for walking me home."

"Anytime. So, are you coming to the party this weekend?" Grayson asked as they stood outside her house.

"What party?"

"We all get together before the big exam and have fun. You should really consider it. It'll be fun. We have one every year."

"It sounds like fun and of course I will have to check with my mom first."

"Right, so um……yeah I guess I will see you later."

"Ok," Jess said as she watched Grayson slowly walk away. What was she thinking. "Hey Grayson," Jess called out. "Would you like to study with us?"

Grayson turned around and smiled. "Sure," he said as he hurried back to where Jess stood.

"Well, this is my house," Jess said as she invited Grayson in.

"Wow," Grayson said as his eyes roamed around the living room. "I always wondered what the inside of a psychotic person's house looked like."

"Seriously?" Jess asked.

"Of course, I wake up thinking about it and go to bed thinking about it," he joked.

"Whatever," Jess said as they both laughed. "You want anything to drink?"

"Yeah sure," he said as he followed Jess into the kitchen.

"Here you go," Jess said as she handed Grayson a soft drink.

"Are you going to show me around?"

"Um...sure. Well this is the kitchen," Jess said with a smile. "You already saw the living room. Here's the bathroom and down the hall there's two bedrooms, two full baths and a half bath."

"That's it? What about that room?" Grayson asked as he pointed towards the door, adjacent to the stairs.

"Oh, that's the basement. I've never been down there."

"How about we go down there together?" Grayson said as he opened the door to the basement. He turns to look at Jess. "What are you waiting on?"

"I'm not going down there," Jess said as she crossed her arms in front of her. "Nothing good ever happens in the basement."

"Well maybe you should come with me so something good can happen," Grayson said right before he disappeared down in the basement.

Jess stood in the doorway. "Grayson!" Jess called out. "I'm not coming down there. Grayson!?" she called out again. This time she figured what the hell. "Ok, fine."

Jess slowly walks down the stairs, stopping on the bottom stair as she looks around. "Grayson, where are you?" she said as she stepped down and began looking around for the light switch.

After feeling around on the wall, Jess finally finds the light switch. As she began to turn the lights on, the hairs on her arms stood up. That feeling of being watched consumed her as she felt Grayson breathing on the back of her neck.

"Grayson, you can't scare me," Jess said in a shaken voice, but there was no answer. "Really? Is this all you have up your sleeve?"

Grayson stood there waiting for Jess to find him until he couldn't take the suspense any longer.

"Who are you talking to?" Grayson questioned as he came from around the corner with a smirk on his face.

Jess looked over and saw Grayson coming from around the corner. She quickly turned back around when she noticed it wasn't Grayson behind her. "I..... I thought you were playing a joke behind me," she said as her voice trembled.

"Um.... no. I've been around the corner waiting on you. Hoping to spook you, but it seems like someone or something beat me to it," he laughed.

"It's not funny Grayson,"

"What? I was over here the entire time. Maybe it was the wind."

Jess wasn't buying that. She knew what the wind felt like. She wasn't fucking crazy.

"Hey, check this out," Grayson said as he held up an old wooden ax.

"Yeah so, it's an ax. What's so special about it?"

"Nothing, but check out the blood on it," Grayson said as he held up the ax to Jess," How cool is that?"

"So gross. There's nothing cool about a bloody ax. Where did you get that from anyway?" Jess said as she crossed her arms.

"Over there," he said as he pointed towards the wall above the work bench.

You could still see the print of the ax on the wall. Jess thought that was odd. Why would a dirty old ax have fresh blood on it? What happened in this house. Maybe the owner had a slaughter house.

"Ok well, put it back and let's just get out of here. Being down here is beginning to creep me out." Jess said as she began heading up the stairs but was pulled back by Grayson as he grabbed her arm.

"Um, what are you doing?" said Jess.

"What do you think I'm doing? I'm trying to make something good happen. You don't have to leave just yet," Grayson said as he pulled Jess closer to him.

Jess placed both of her hands up in front of her to keep Grayson from pulling her closer.

"Look, we need to get going. Friends are coming over, remember?" said Jess.

"I'm sure they can wait," Grayson said as he tried to pull Jess even closer, but Jess wouldn't budge. "What are you afraid of?"

"I'm not afraid of anything, I just want to get back upstairs," Jess said right before the doorbell rang. "Looks like they are here."

Grayson released Jess from his grasp as she hurried upstairs. He stood there for a minute before heading upstairs. It wasn't that he was scared, but he just didn't want Jess to see the disappointment on his face. He was always used to getting what he wanted, except for this time.

"Hurry up and open the door," Becca yelled.

"I'm coming," Jess said right before she opened the door.

"Gosh what took you so long?" Becca said as she walked right pass Jess. Followed by Meghan and Alaina.

"I was busy getting something to drink," said Jess.

Jess couldn't stand Alaina. Ever since the day they met, Alaina seemed to have such an attitude with Jess. She didn't know why. All she knew was to not trust Alaina.

"Hey Jess," Meghan said.

"Hey," said Jess.

Jess didn't bother to speak to Alaina.

"Bitch you don't have to speak to me," said Alaina.

"Great, at least we both agree on something," Jess said right as Grayson walked into the living room.

Everyone turned to look at Grayson.

"Well, I guess we all know why she took so long answering the door," Alaina said with a smirk on her face. "Busy with Grayson."

"What? Nothing happened." Jess said. She was about fed up with Alaina's hateful ways.

"Just like nothing happened when you locked me in the bathroom," Alaina said as she moved closer to Jess.

"I didn't lock you in the bathroom. How many times do I have to say it!"

"Yeah whatever. I better not catch you alone," said Alaina.

"Or what?" she asked.

"You'll find out. It wouldn't be the first time someone's come up missing."

Everyone looked at Alaina. Someone needed to do something before she said too much.

"What are you talking about?" said Jess.

"Nothing," Becca said while staring at Alaina." Look you guys, we are here to study."

"I'm not going upstairs in this freaks bedroom," Alaina said as she glared at Jess. "I'm staying downstairs." She didn't like Jess and it showed.

Alaina crossed her arms and flopped down on the couch. She was determined not to get along with Jess. She didn't like her, and she had her reasons.

"Can we please just get started," Meghan said as she took a seat as well. "Some people do have a life outside of school and studying."

Everyone took a seat and began studying. The room was quiet. For a while no one said anything. They continued to study in silence until the silence was interrupted by a knock on the door. Everyone looked at each other.

"Well don't look at us, this isn't our house," said Alaina as she rolled her eyes.

"Actually. It's for me," Grayson said as he jumped up from the chair he was sitting in and walked to the door.

"Hey what's up guys, Where's

Jeffery?" Grayson said as he opened the door and gave his friends Todd and Desmond the cool hand shake.

"Jeffery had a meeting with the Debate Club." Desmond said as he walked in. "I'm telling you man, Jeffery is doing more than debating. Who has three Debate meetings in a week? And who and what are they debating?"

"I don't think that's it," said Todd. "I heard his mom doesn't want him hanging around us anymore. But too bad for him, he's missing out on all the fun."

Todd, Grayson and Desmond have been friends since the beginning of middle school. The cool guys that most wanted to be, and half couldn't stand. They were all on the football team. Jeffery was the newcomer that joined the group of friends. Whenever it was time to hang out, he would make up an excuse to not hang out with them. Ever since that day at the party.

"We're in here studying or should I say, they are studying. Did you bring the booze?"

"Of course, don't I always come through." Todd replied as they all follow

Grayson through the foyer and into the living room.

"Hope you didn't mind me inviting a few friends over," Grayson said as he sat next to Jess.

"I don't mind, but you could have asked, we are trying to study you know," Jess said as she tapped her pen on her notebook.

"Don't mind us, we're just chilling," said Desmond.

"Is that alcohol?" Jess asked Grayson.

"Yeah, it's not a big deal," said Todd as he glanced around.

"Ok and who are you?"

"This is Todd," Grayson said as he introduced them. "He's on the football team too."

Jess could care less what team either one of them were on right about now. If her mom walked in and saw alcohol she would be in big trouble.

"Can I like talk to you for a minute?" Jess asked Grayson as she stood up.

"Sure," Grayson said as he remained seated.

"In the kitchen." Jess said as she headed to the kitchen and waited for Grayson.

Minutes later Grayson stood in the kitchen leaning against the counter. "You needed to see me for what?"

"Grayson, you know I can't have alcohol in the house. If my mom finds out she will kill me," said Jess.

"She won't find out. Who's going to tell her anyway?" Grayson asked as he searched for a bottle opener.

"What if she walks in?" Jess asked as she stood there and watched Grayson search for the bottle opener.

"If she walks in I will say you had nothing to do with it."

"Yeah just like you didn't say anything when Alaina was trying to assume something was going on between us?" Jess asked.

Grayson stopped and looked at Jess but didn't say anything.

"Nothing to say?" said Jess.

"What do you want me to say Jess?" said Grayson.

"I don't know. Maybe, you could start off with an apology or maybe say something to her? Now she's probably going to tell everyone that I sleep around. Then my mom will be upset with me."

"She wouldn't do something like that," he said.

"You don't know that," said Jess.

He gave up his search for the bottle opener. "Well I guess the apple don't fall too far from the tree then," Grayson said as he took one of the knives out of the drawer. "This will work."

He left Jess standing there with his words lingering in her head. Apparently, everyone knows her mom's past, except for her.

"We're taking this party down in the basement," Grayson said as he interrupted Jess's thoughts.

She reached over and placed the bottle opener on the counter and decided to call her mom to see when she was coming home before shit got out of hand.

"Who are you calling?" Grayson asked as he entered the kitchen with his friends.

"My mom. I was trying to see when she was coming home. You know, so I can give a heads up whenever she's near," Jess said as she eased her phone into her back pocket.

"Well, you ladies can study while me and the boys are going to study in the basement," Grayson said as he held up one of the six packs of beer, trailing behind his friends as they made their way into the basement.

"Yo where's the light?" said Desmond. "What kind of basement doesn't have a light man."

"Dude, it's on the wall when you get to the bottom." said Grayson. "There on the right."

"Man, this is straight out a horror movie type shit here," Desmond said as he searched for the light switch. "Trying to get a brother killed. You know we always die first in the movies."

"Dude, chill out," Grayson laughed. "Just turn the fucking light on."

"I don't see the fucking light," Desmond replied.

Grayson made his way around Desmond and Todd and searched for the light switch. "Finally," he said as he flipped the switch. "You guys are chickens."

"Oh yeah? Don't say anything when we have to save your ass," Desmond said as he took a seat on the bottom of the stairs. "Dude no wonder you are quiet."

"I only took a couple puffs," Todd said as he took another puff from his blunt before handing it to Grayson.

"You know we have practice tomorrow?" said Grayson.

"It's just one blunt. So... you going to let my hand fall off or are you going to take a hit?"

"Dude, nobody wants to lose their scholarships and their damn lungs," said Desmond.

"Exactly. Plus, if coach finds out, he will kick us off the team and I don't need my parents riding my ass," Grayson said as he popped opened a few beer bottles and handed them off to his friends.

"I thought your mom left your dad?" Todd asked.

"She's a flight attendant. So technically she leaves him every other day," Grayson replied.

"Yo, you ask too many questions when you are high," said Desmond.

Grayson found an old rusty fold out chair in the corner, dragged it back where his friends were and took a seat, while Todd sat next to Desmond. They talked and talked until the minutes flew by and drank until Grayson was tipsy. He no longer occupied the chair he was sitting in. He sat on the floor where his back rested against the side of the stairs.

"Yo Grayson, what's up with you and your girl Jess?" Todd asked, who was too high to hold his head up.

"She's not my girl. She wouldn't even put out," said Grayson. "The only girl to turn down these good looks."

"She's not the only girl," said Desmond.

That comment made Grayson get up from the floor and stare at Desmond. As if he wanted to say something.

"Yo check out this bloody ax I saw earlier," Grayson said as he staggered over towards the wall. "It's got blood all over it. I wonder who….," Grayson began to say, but lost his words.

"Bro what's wrong? Cat's got your tongue?" Desmond said as he made his way beside Grayson.

"There was an ax here. Right here," he said as he walked closer towards the work bench and pointed at the wall. "Right here. I swear it was right here."

"What was right there?" Desmond asked.

"The ax and it's…. it's gone," he stuttered.

CHAPTER NINE

Claire pulled up in front of an older house, it was gorgeous. Old, but beautiful with charm.

"Twenty-eight fifty-four Woodard Lane," Claire read out loud before gathering her phone and purse.

She eased out of her car and looked around. The feeling of being followed haunted her as she made her way up the driveway towards the house, still looking back to make sure she wasn't being followed.

She slowly made her way on the porch, took a deep breath and knocked. There was no answer, so she knocked again. She reached in her purse and checked the address again before ringing the doorbell. Still no answer. She glanced through the window, hoping to see someone moving inside, but instead she saw nothing. She gave it one final knock with no luck and decided to leave.

Claire was halfway down the steps when she heard a voice call out to her.

"Who are you? What are you doing here?" she said.

"Peggy?" Claire asked as she turned around to a door half cracked open. "Peggy Woolrich?"

"Who wants to know?"

"Oh, I'm sorry," Claire said as she carefully made her way back towards the door.

"Don't come any closer or I will blow your fucking head off," she threatened.

Claire was no fool. Too scared to go any closer, she did as she was told, and she stopped dead in her tracks. "I'm Claire Vanderbilt, I bought your previous house."

"Yeah and? What are you doing here?"

"I wanted to talk to you about your daughter," Claire said as she looked around.

"What about my daughter?" Peggy asked as she opened the door a little wider.

"Could we maybe talk inside Ms.

Woolrich. I promise I won't take up much of your time," Claire begged.

Peggy cracked opened the door even more wider than before.

Claire was happy she was making a little progress. "Every little bit counts," Claire thought to herself, until she heard a gun being cocked and was now looking down the barrel of a shotgun. She was now speechless.

"You have three seconds to get the hell off my property," Peggy said furiously and began counting. "One," she yelled.

"Ms. Woolrich I just want to talk about your daughter. It's very important," Claire said in a shaky voice.

"There's nothing you can tell me about my daughter that I don't already know," Peggy yelled as she continued counting. "Two."

Claire was running out of time. She should leave, but she needed answers. She needed to think of something quick to change Peggy's mind.

Just as Peggy counted to three, Claire

closed her eyes and yells out, "I believe I saw your daughter!"

Everything went silent. Claire opened her eyes and released the breath of air she was holding. She was alive in one piece. No longer looking down the barrel of a shot gun, but instead looking at Peggy. Starring directly into her worried blue eyes.

"What do you mean you saw my daughter?" Peggy asked. Even though she was no longer pointing the gun at Claire, she was still holding on to it.

"The day my daughter and I arrived in town…...a girl walked in front of my car. I didn't know who she was at the time until Officer Bradley showed me a picture," Claire stated.

"Officer Bradley," Peggy repeated.

"If I can come in I promise I can explain everything that's been happening?" Claire asked.

Peggy was hesitant at first, but she needed to hear whatever it was that involved her daughter. She needed some closure. Ever since the disappearance of her daughter Sarah, Peggy spends most of her days at home. Mingling was a thing of the past. She just wanted her daughter back.

She didn't say a word. She just opened her door and signal for Claire to come in.

"Thank you," Claire said.

Peggy quickly glanced around one last time before closing the door behind her.

"May I take your jacket?" Peggy asked.

"No thank you, I won't be long," Claire said as she followed Peggy into the living room. She stopped to admire the family photos on the wall, mostly of Peggy and her daughter Sarah. She also noticed the numerous amounts of crosses on the wall. She thought that was a little strange as she stood there and stared.

"The crosses, they keep away the evil spirits. You can have a seat," said Peggy.

"You have a lovely home," Claire said as she took a seat in a chair. "What made you move here?"

Peggy wrapped her pale-yellow sweater cardigan around her small frame and took a seat on the end of the sofa.

"I miss my baby girl. She was all that I had. Then he…... some monster took her from me," Peggy sobbed.

Claire reached over and grabbed Peggy's hands. "I would be lying if I said I understand what you are going through, because I don't, but I can only imagine. The day will come when justice will seek revenge."

Peggy didn't say a word. She just held on to Claire's hands until her tears slowly subsided. It's been a while since she shared her feelings about her daughter. It was a sense of relief to have someone to talk to.

"Everywhere I turned I felt Sarah's presence, so I moved here. Sometimes it seems as if she was in the house. I often would hear someone crying and calling out for help. Windows were often found open throughout the house, especially in a Sarah's room. There would also be this terrible smell that would come and go. I didn't know what it was at first, but then I realized it must have been someone or an evil spirit," said Peggy.

Saying those words had Claire

thinking about the times she wondered how the windows were left open and that smell was the same smell she would often smell around the house too. She didn't bother tell Jess, afraid that it would have alarm her.

Peggy said as she stared at a picture of her daughter on the wall. "Why are you here?"

"My daughter, she's been having dreams of your daughter. She wakes up crying and scared. At first, I thought they were just dreams, but everything is starting to add up," said Claire.

She reached in her purse and pulled out several photos. "These are photos of…."

"Sarah's old room," Peggy said as she interrupted Claire. "What happened?"

"We went out shopping and came home to this. The detective said it didn't appear to be a break in, but they will investigate it," said Claire.

Peggy sat quietly as she went through each photo. "Unfriend Me," she said quietly to herself. "Those words… Sarah was big on anti-bullying, she wanted to start a non-profit organization to help those who were being bullied like herself."

"Do you remember what she said? Anything from that day?" Claire asked.

"I didn't want her to go, but she was so happy to finally be invited to a party with the cool kids," Peggy said as the thought of her daughter crosses her mind, causing her to smile. Her smile quickly vanished when she realized her daughter wasn't coming home. "She said she would just unfriend them."

"Unfriend them how? By social media?" Claire asked.

"No, Sarah wasn't into social media. She was a good kid. She didn't bother anyone. She just wanted to fit in," said Peggy as she continued looking through the photos. "Is this your daughter?" she asked.

"Yes," she replied.

"She's beautiful and perfect," said Peggy.

"Thank you. Jess, she's my only daughter too. She didn't want to move here, but she's adjusting well," Claire said as she stared at her daughter in the picture.

"That necklace, Sarah was wearing the same necklace that day she left the house," Peggy said as she looked closer at the photo.

"Are you sure? Maybe... it's just a coincidence or something," said Claire.

"No. I had it made for her sixteenth birthday," Peggy stated.

Claire continued staring at the photo. Her concerns grew even greater. Wondering if her daughter could be in any harm.

"I need to go. I've taken up enough of your time," Claire said as she grabbed her purse and stood up to leave.

"Was it something I said?" Peggy asked.

"No." Claire lied. "I have somewhere else to be but thank you for your time." She anxiously walked to the door with Peggy walking behind her.

Once she reached the door and opened it, she stopped and turned towards Peggy. She could tell her heart was still heavy. "Peggy, I want to find out what happened to your daughter. I promise, when I do, you will be the first to know," Claire said.

She then reached out and gave Peggy a hug. She would do everything she could to find out what happened to Sarah Woolrich.

Peggy held back the tears as she hugged Claire back. "Only the unspoken and disturbed spirits visit ones in their sleep. She's out for revenge," Peggy whispered as Claire slowly let go.

Claire looked at Peggy, wondering what she meant. "What are you talking about?" Claire asked.

"Thank you for stopping by," Peggy said before closing the door. She left Claire standing there on the porch trying to figure out what exactly did you mean.

"What does that mean?" she called out as she knocked on the door. "Is my daughter in trouble? Peggy! Peggy please!" she yelled, hoping Peggy would return to the door, but there was no answer.

The clouds began to roll in as the sky turned darker. The rain began to fall. Claire hurried down the squeaky steps, ran to her car, unlocked her door and got in. She looked up towards the house she just left as the words out of Peggy's mouth lingered on her mind.

She reached into her purse for her phone, two missed calls from her daughter. Was something wrong? She then began calling her daughter back, but there was no answer. She called again, this time leaving a voicemail. "Jess sweetie, pick up the phone. I need to know you're ok."

Claire tried to stay calm. She didn't want to upset her daughter. Did she have her friends over? Was she hurt and calling for her mom's help? So many questions went through her mind as she gave up calling and decided to just head home. She tossed her phone back in her purse and threw her purse aside, causing it to land in the passenger seat.

Home was a little over half an hour away. The rain continued to fall harder and harder, blinding Claire's view. She should pull over, but she needed to get home to see Jess and to make sure she was ok.

"Geeze you're fucking blinding me!" Claire yelled while throwing up her right hand. Giving the driver in the pickup truck behind her the middle finger. She adjusted her rearview mirror, but it was no match for what was about to happen next.

The truck came closer and closer. The closer it came, the brighter it's lights beamed into Claire's car. They were now bumper to bumper.

"Fucking asshole!" Claire yelled as she sped up, increasing her speed while the truck trailed her. Her old car was no match for the heavy-duty pickup truck behind her. Whomever it was blew their horn like a crazy person.

Sensing something was wrong, Claire reached for her purse while trying to keep an eye on the road. She needed her phone, to call for help. After fumbling around in her purse Claire finally retrieves her phone and began dialing 911. At that moment the truck behind her slams into her, causing her to drop her phone, as her car skids across the road.

"Oh my God!" Claire screamed and panic as she looked back at the truck that was coming for her again.

Her phone was on the floor of her car, near her right foot. She looked down and reached for it but couldn't grab it.

"Damn it!" she yelled. Frustration and fear was setting in, causing her to panic even more. She needed to think quickly. She took her left foot and slid the phone towards her, just enough so that she could reach it. Claire took another glimpse back at the truck riding her bumper before reaching down again. "Yes!" she yells in joy, but she spoke too early.

Right as she was reaching down to pick up her phone, the engine roared and roared louder and louder from the truck behind her as it slammed into the back of her car again causing her to drop her phone again. She struggled to maintain control of her car. She looks back at the truck behind her again before looking at the road, suddenly slamming on the brakes to avoid hitting the human figure standing in the middle of the road.

"Oh my gosh!!" she screams as she lost control of her car and slides off the road and down into a steep ditch, before coming to a complete stop. Then there was silence.

The only thing you could hear was the car horn sounding endlessly, while the car lights flickered against the night.

911 Operator: 911 what's your emergency? Hello? Caller are you ok?......Stay on the line, help is on the way.

CHAPTER TEN

Jess and her friends sat quietly while they studied. It was getting late and she hadn't heard back from her mom.

Alaina was getting inpatient, she didn't want to be there from the beginning. "I'm going home. I've done enough studying for tonight," Alaina said as she grabbed her backpack.

"She's right," said Becca. "It's getting late. We should all leave together."

"I'm fine. I can walk alone," Alaina said as she walked towards the front door.

"How about I walk you home?" Todd asked as he got up from the chair he was sitting in.

"I don't need a fucking babysitter. I'll be fine," Alaina replied then walked out the door.

"Give her a few minutes and follow her Todd," said Becca.

Todd pretended to clear his throat, "I believe she stated she didn't need a fucking babysitter."

Becca looked at Todd, before looking at Grayson. Who was sitting on the couch beside Jess. "I think it's getting to her. She's been acting paranoid and weird lately. Someone needs to walk her home"

"What's getting to her?" Jess asked.

"Nothing," said Grayson as he got up from the couch and walked towards Todd. "Do me this favor and follow her. Just make sure she gets home safe. She doesn't have to know you're following her."

"Gosh! Fine, I'll do it just this time," Todd said as he opened the door.

"Don't try anything," Grayson whispered.

"Yeah sure," Todd said as he turned and looked at Grayson before closing the door.

Grayson turned around and everyone was staring at him, "What?" he questioned.

"We're going to go ahead and leave.

Desmond is walking us home," said Meghan who has been quiet most of the day.

"Are you coming with us?" Becca asked.

"Um...you guys can go ahead. I'll catch up with you all tomorrow at school," Grayson said as he stood there with his hands in his pockets.

"Alright dude, peace out," Desmond says out loud as he, Meghan and Becca walk out the door.

"Ok, you're staying behind because of what? To explain to me your involvement with Alaina?" Jess said as immediately after the door was closed.

"We are just friends," he replied.

"Bullshit. I'm not stupid Grayson. Do you see the way she looks at me whenever I'm talking to you?!" Jess yells.

"I swear we are nothing, but close friends. We've known each other since kindergarten. We became good friends. We made a promise to each other." Grayson knew that was the wrong thing to say and regretted saying it. Those words made him looked even more guiltier than before. He didn't know what to say. This was a compromising situation for him. If only she would understand.

"A promise? What kind of promise?" said Jess as she waited for Grayson to answer, but no answer. "I need to finish up some things, you can see your way out," she said as she storms off towards the kitchen with him right behind her.

"Jess… it isn't like that," Grayson rambled as he reached out for Jess.

"Well, then tell me…I'm waiting," she said as she stood with her arms crossed.

Grayson stood there for a minute, trying to choose his words carefully. "We made a promise to always be there for each other. We've been friends since day one."

"You sound like a broken record Grayson," she said. "I don't think you can hear yourself talk. No, I don't think you even realize the words that come out of your mouth."

"Jess it's the truth, I swear."

"And you want me to believe that? Out of everything that happened tonight, I'm supposed to believe that?"

"Look I know that it doesn't sound right, but all I ask is that you trust me," he begged.

"Trust you? I trusted that you would say something earlier, but instead you made me look like a complete whore," Jess said as she picked up her cellphone off the counter and saw missed calls from her mom. Without checking her voicemail, she immediately calls back.

"Um who are you calling?" Grayson asked nervously.

"Don't worry, I'm not calling the cops," said Jess. She could see Grayson exhaling, which made her wonder. Why was he nervous? There was something he wasn't telling her. "Unfortunately, you can't get arrested for being a lying asshole."

Jess looked away and began trying to call her mom, but there was no answer. She hung up and tried again. Still no answer. She started to get worried.

"What's wrong?" Grayson asked. He could see the look on Jess's face. She was worried about something.

"I can't reach my mom. It went straight to voicemail."

"Maybe she's busy, if you know what I mean," Grayson said with a sly grin on his face.

"I don't know what you are insinuating, but if it's what I think…It's not funny. Plus, my mom never turns her phone off," she said as she placed her phone back on the kitchen counter and began slowly pacing the floor.

"Sorry, I was only joking. Did she leave a voicemail?"

Jess stopped pacing the floor and looked up at Grayson. "I don't know, I didn't bother to check." She grabs her phone and sees a notification at the very top and began dialing her voicemail. She places the phone against her ear and started to panic. "Something's wrong."

"What did she say?" he asked.

"She just wanted to make sure I was ok, but she sounded differently."

"There's nothing wrong with that," here replied.

"You don't know my mom," Jess said as she stared at Grayson. "She sounded like something was wrong." Jess tried calling her mom again. "She's not answering. It's still going straight to her voicemail."

"I'm sure she's ok. She can take care of herself," said Grayson. He knew he had said the wrong thing when Jess gave him that get lost look. "Look I'm sorry. I know you are worried and...."

"Just leave," said Jess. "Go check on Alaina or something."

"She's not my girlfriend!" Grayson said as his voice got louder. He was getting frustrated. Maybe he should just tell her. Would she even believe him?

"Look Grayson, it's getting late and I have better things to do. Like find out where my mom is. So, please just leave. I'm sure Alaina would be heartbroken if she found out you were still here," Jess said as she grabbed her phone off the counter and began walking away towards the living room.

"She wouldn't be heartbroken because she's not my girlfriend! She's my sister!" Grayson yells as he cups his face in the palm of his hands. Causing Jess to stop in her tracks and turn to look at him.

"What do you mean she's your sister?" she questioned.

"It's a long story."

"I don't believe you."

"What?" Grayson was afraid this would happen. "Which part don't you believe? The long story or the whole story?"

"The whole story. I'm sure if she was your sister, she would have mentioned it. They all would have mentioned it."

"They didn't mention it because…."

Just as Grayson was about to explain the doorbell rung, followed by a knock. They both looked at each other, wondering who it could be. The knock came again and again.

"I'll go with you," he said.

"Ok… thanks." She accepted his kind gesture, but still didn't believe a word he said.

Slowly and carefully they both walked to the door.

"I'll open it, just stand behind me,"

Grayson insisted.

"Ok," Jess said as she nodded her head.

The knocking continued. Finally, Grayson placed his hand on the door and looked at Jess and slightly opened the door.

"Dad?" Grayson said as he opened the door wider.

"Grayson? What are you doing here?" Grayson's dad asked.

"I was studying with a few friends here. What are you doing here?"

"I'm here to see Jess, it's about her mother Claire."

Jess didn't bother to wait any longer. She sprung from around the door with fear in her eyes. "What about my mother? What happened? Is she ok?" The tears began to form in Jess's eyes.

"You need to come with me, she's been in an accident," Officer Bradley stated.

Jess grabbed her blue purse from off the couch and hurried out the door.

CHAPTER ELEVEN

The rain continued to fall as Alaina walked as fast as she could. She only stayed three blocks over, but the rain made her walk seem longer. She held her messenger style book bag above her head, shielding herself from the rain as she walked the dark streets.

"Gosh, I knew I should have left early. I could have beaten this stupid rain," she said to herself.

No one else was around as her feet slapped against the wet pavement, causing water to splash even more.

"Shit," Alaina said as water soaked the bottom of her blue jeans.

After walking for another five minutes, she reached her quiet block. "Finally," she said quietly as she stopped at the corner of a tall brick fence and looked down at her pants legs. They were soaked. She made it about five feet before deciding to do something quick about her soaked jeans.

The rain seemed to be letting up. Alaina took this time to squeeze the water out of the hem of her jeans.

As she bent down and began squeezing the water out, she heard a noise that sounded like footsteps. Footsteps that wasn't hers. She quickly looked around.

"Hello?" Alaina calls out. Her voice was shaky. She wasn't the type to get scared, but she was scared as hell. Lately paranoia has been riding her ass just as sure as the daylight. Ever since the disappearance of Sarah, the guilt has been taking a toll on Alaina. Sarah didn't deserve to be treated like that. Things just got out of hand. She could have saved her, but she didn't. Now, all she could see was the vision of Sarah's face haunting her. She wished that she could escape her thoughts, but there was no escaping.

Alaina stood up and looked around again... she saw no one. "Hello?" she calls out again. "Anyone there?"

She walks slowly and carefully towards the direction in which she had just come from. The damp air made her wish she had brought along her jacket. She walked a few feet towards the corner, when she saw a shadow from behind that startled her even more.

"Who's there? I know someone's there. I can see your shadow," said Alaina.

She reached into her bag for something to use as a weapon and quickly withdrew an ink pen. She looked at it, it wasn't a weapon, but it was all that she had, and this would have to do.

"Are you hurt? I…I can help you… if you need help," she calls out, but still no answer.

She didn't know what was lurking around the wall, but she was going to find out. She was tired of living in the shadows of the past. She didn't know what was real and what was not anymore. She had nothing to lose. It was all or nothing.

Alaina took a deep breath. "You can do this," she said to herself as she jumped out from around the corner. She saw someone running and that someone was Todd.

"Todd!?" she yells causing Todd to stop running.

He stops and throws his hands up. "Alright, alright you caught me," Todd said as he turned around and walked back to the corner where Alaina stood.

"You creep! You could have given me a heart attack!"

"Shhh keep your voice down. Are you trying to wake up the whole damn neighborhood?" Todd questioned.

"Maybe I should. So, everyone will know that this creep was stalking me."

"I wasn't stalking you alright. They wanted me to follow you. You know...make sure you got home ok."

"Who are they?" Alaina asked.

"Grayson and your friends. They care about you. They're just looking out for you," Todd said with sincerity in his voice.

"Oh really? They're looking out for me? How so? The last time I checked, you were running away from me like little a bitch," Alaina said with a sly grin.

"That's enough Alaina. I didn't want you to catch me because I knew how you would react and I was right."

Alaina moved closer to Todd, causing him to take a step back, "You don't know anything, and you definitely do not know me."

"You haven't been thinking straight lately and you won't talk to us. We're your friends."

"I can take care of myself. I don't need your sympathy or anyone else," Alaina said as she looked around as if someone was watching her.

"There's no one there Alaina," said Todd as he stared at Alaina.

"I gotta go. She's coming."

Alaina left Todd standing there, wondering who was the "she", Alaina was referring to.

"Alaina wait," Todd said as he caught up to her. "What are you talking about?"

"She's coming, I gotta go," she said as she was about to take off again but was stopped when Todd grabbed her right arm.

"Who's coming? You're not making any sense here," Todd stated. "What's going on with you?" He questioned with a grin.

"Sarah...she's coming," said Alaina.

His grin slowly faded. Todd could see how terrified she was and how her voice crackled with fear. She was serious as ever.

"Alaina, Sarah's not coming for you. Trust me," he reassured her.

Alaina snatched her arm away. "She's coming. She's coming for all of us. She wants revenge," Alaina said as she ran off as fast as she could.

Alaina was four houses away from her home. She ran as fast as her legs could carry her. She didn't bother to look back to see if Todd followed her. Once inside she took a deep breath and rested her back against the door. She glanced out the window before quietly heading upstairs. Trying not to wake her mom, she eased open her bedroom door and closed it behind her.

Thank goodness everyone was asleep. Alaina stayed with her mom Doris and her younger brother Ethan who is seven. Her step father Ray once stayed with them. He was a good father until a year ago. One day he just up and left. He said he was going to the store and never came back. They never saw him again.

It was getting late. Alaina took her shower and headed to bed. Another school day tomorrow, along with an exam. She needed rest and needed it right away.

She laid her head down on her pillow and pulled the covers over her body and slipped her head under. She exhaled and closed her eyes. Maybe tomorrow will be different. Hopefully tomorrow will be better.

Hours had passed. Alaina tossed and turned most of the night. She just couldn't sleep. Every time she closed her eyes, she kept seeing Sarah. The dreams seemed so real, as if she was right in the room with her.

"What's wrong with me?" she whispers to herself. Then suddenly her body became still, as the sound of her bedroom door slowly creeped open.

Alaina quietly pulled her bed covers even more over her head. Trying to hide from whomever just walked in, she closed her eyes and began praying.

"Please God, please don't let me die," Alaina cried silently to herself as the footsteps came closer. "Oh God," she whispers, while keeping her eyes shut. She tried her best to remain still and calm, but her trembling body gave her away.

She could feel the presence of someone standing next to her bed. Her heart began to race and beat faster than it has ever been before. In her mind, she began saying her prayers repeatedly.

"Please go away, just go away...please." she cried silently to herself as she felt a hand resting on her left shoulder, followed by a soft voice.

"Alaina," the voice called out.

Alaina laid there still as a rock, not wanting to move. Afraid of what would happen if she did.

"Alaina," the voice called out again.

"Ethan?" Alaina asked curiously as she slowly removed the bed covers from off her head. There standing at her bed side was her little brother. A sigh of relief escaped her body. "Ethan, what are you doing out of bed?"

"I can't sleep. There's a monster in my closet," Ethan said as he held his stuffed teddy bear.

Alaina sat up in her bed. "There's no such thing as a monster Ethan," she said as she brushed away the two tiny curls that laid against his forehead.

"Yes there is and it's in my closet," Ethan whined. "I don't wanna sleep in there. Can I sleep in here with you?"

"How about I go and check things out," Alaina said as she pulled the covers from off her legs and began to walk towards the door.

"No please don't go, she will get you," Ethan said as he grabbed hold of his sister's hand and tried to pull her back, causing Alaina to stop.

She turned to Ethan to reassure him that everything was ok and not to be scared. Deep down inside she was scared but needed to be strong for him.

"Ok. You can sleep with me tonight," Alaina said as Ethan wrapped his small arms around her legs.

Ethan ran to Alaina's bed and jumped in. Alaina did the same. She reached over and tucked him in.

"Alaina," Ethan whispered softly.

"Yes Ethan," Alaina answered.

"You're the best sister ever. I love you."

Alaina smiled. She loved her brother. "I love you too Ethan. Thanks for being the best brother a sister could ask for."

Ethan smiled and drifted off to sleep, while Alaina stayed awake. Something that Ethan had said seemed to ponder on her mind. Who was "she", Ethan was referring to? Did he see Sarah too? So many questions left unanswered. She wanted to ask him, but she didn't want to frighten him even more.

After making sure Ethan was sound asleep, Alaina eased out of the bed and out of her bedroom. She carefully closed her bedroom door. She didn't want to wake Ethan. She knew if he woke up, he would be totally against her going. She wanted to make sure monsters really didn't exist.

Alaina reached her brother's room. She placed her hand on the door and took a deep breath. She would be quick. They only had an hour and a half left, before it was time to get up and get ready for school. She eased the door open. Her eyes wandered the room before fully walking in. Nothing seemed out of the ordinary. Then her eyes rested on the closet. She slowly walks to it, then closed her eyes and prayed nothing was there before yanking open the doors.

Alaina's heart skipped a beat, but there was nothing there. She was smiling at the thought of monsters really being in a closet.

"See, no monsters in your closet Ethan," she said silently to herself. Alaina was smiling as she closed the closet door, but that smile soon faded as she turned around.

She let out a blood screeching scream, before her throat was sliced opened. She grabbed her neck with both hands, trying to stop the bleeding before falling to her knees.

"You're not Sarah," she managed to whisper as the tears slid down her face. "So, this is how it feels to die," she thought to herself, before closing her eyes as her world went dark.

CHAPTER TWELVE

Jess waited in the lobby area of Cloverville Hospital, facing the windows while barely staying awake. She was hoping to see her mom soon, whom was still in surgery.

"Jess?" a male voice called out.

Jess looked around to see who was calling her name. "Detective Armstrong, what are you doing here?" she asked.

"I came to see how your mom was doing," he said before taking a seat next to Jess.

"She's still in surgery," Jess said sadly.

"Yeah, that's what I was told," said Detective Armstrong. He could see the sadness in Jess's eyes and voice. She was worried about her mother. They both were. "Hey," he said as Jess looked at him. "Everything's going to be alright."

"Yeah...I know," she replied then

looked away.

"Jessica Vanderbilt," a nurse calls out.

Both Jess and Detective Armstrong turned around to look at the female nurse.

"Jessica?" the nurse asked.

"Yes, that's me," she replied as she got up and walked towards the nurse. Detective Armstrong followed, but stayed a few feet behind. "How's my mom? Is she ok?"

"She's out of surgery. That's all I can say for now, but I will need for you to follow me," the nurse said with a reassuring smile as she led Jess out of the waiting room and into another room that read "Family Waiting Room."

"Why am I going in here?" Jess asked nervously as they stood outside of the room. "Doesn't everyone that goes in here, receive bad news?"

"Not everyone," the nurse said as she held open the door. "It's just a more private place for doctors to discuss the outcome of the patients with their loved ones."

Jess glanced inside the room. Inside

were two small tan leather couches, along with a small writing table pushed up against the wall accompanied by a chair. "Ok," she said.

The nurse looked at Detective Armstrong. "You must be the husband?"

"NO," Jess and Detective Armstrong both said at the same time as they looked at each other.

"He's not my mom's husband," said Jess.

"I'm just a close friend of the family," he stated.

The nurse looked from Detective Armstrong to Jess.

"It's ok he can stay. I don't mind him hearing whatever the doctor has to say. I'm sure that's what my mom would want," Jess said as they had a seat inside of the room.

"Ok. Well make yourselves at home. The doctor will be in shortly to further discuss your mom's status. If you need any assistance or have any questions, the nurse's station is right around the corner and the breakroom is right past the nurse's station."

"Thank you, "Detective Armstrong said.

The nurse smiled and closed the door. Jess was already asleep on the couch. It wasn't top notch comfort, but it sure beats sleeping on some hard chairs.

"Is she gone yet?" Jess whispered in a sleepy voice.

"Yeah, she's gone and if she wasn't, I think she would have heard you," he said as he laughed.

"Yeah whatever," she said.

"You know, you try to play tough and hard, but you have a soft exterior," Detective Armstrong stated.

"Who said anything about trying to play hard. I'm tired, sleepy, hungry and I've been waiting forever to see my mom," she said as she sat up on the couch. "I just want to see my mom. She's all I have here."

"Yeah I know what you mean. Some years ago, in my patrol days my partner was here in the hospital."

"What happened to him?" Jess asked.

Detective Armstrong looked down in his hands. "He was shot. We responded to a stolen car call. The passenger had a gun. Everything happened so fast. He was rushed to the hospital. The family and I…we waited and waited. Seconds turned into minutes. Minutes turned into hours."

"I'm sorry about your partner," Jess said.

"No worries. He's back to his old self again," Detective Armstrong said as he smiled. I'm going to go see what I can find for us to snack on."

"Ok," Jess said just before he left out of the room. Jess laid back down and stared into empty space.

She was tired and needed to rest but didn't want to fall asleep. At least not now. She wanted to be awake and alert for when the doctor comes in. She tried her best to fight the sleep that was consuming her, but eventually she gave in.

She began tossing and turning. Her dreams began taunting her again. In her dreams sat a crying girl, with her back against a tree. Jess tried to see who it was, but the tree was blocking her sight.

"Hello. Are you ok?" Jess calls out as she walks closer towards the tree.

The girl continues to cry. Something was wrong. Was she hurt? Who was she? Could this be Sarah?

"Sarah? Sarah Woolrich?" Jess calls out. Instantly the girl stopped crying. "Sarah what happened to you?"

The girl said nothing. Suddenly, a burst of laughter erupted from her. "They will pay for what they did. Confess or they will all die," she whispers before laughing again.

"What are you talking about? What happened to you?" Jess asked as she now stood right behind the tree.

Then there was silence again. No laughter...no crying. She continued sitting still as a rock with her back against the tree.

Jess looked up in the sky, a storm was coming. "Sarah," Jess whispers before bending down on both knees beside Sarah. She reached out and touched Sarah's shoulder, but no response. "Sarah it's ok. I will help you."

The wind began to pick up. Jess reached out again and slightly shook Sarah's shoulder causing her to fall over onto her side, revealing the left side of her face. Something was wrong.

She lifts Sarah into her arms, causing her head to fall towards her chest, revealing her entire face. Jess gasp at the sight of Sarah's face. "Oh my gosh Sarah!" she said franticly. "Who did this to you?"

Sarah's body slowly began to deteriorate right before Jess's eyes. The odor was so strong, causing Jess to cough uncontrollably. She felt a hand on her shoulder shaking her. Someone was calling her name.

"Jess wake up. Wake up Jess," Detective Armstrong said as he lightly shook Jess, trying to wake her up. "Jess, Jess wake up."

Jess slowly opened her eyes. "What happened?" she asked through her groggy voice.

"You were dreaming and apparently

not a good dream." Detective Armstrong said.

"The doctor," Jess said as she sat up on the couch. "Did the doctor come in yet?"

"No not yet," he stated.

"How long have I been asleep?" she asked as she looked around for a clock.

"I've only been gone for about ten minutes. I just walked in, so I'm guessing not long," he said before taking a seat where he was sitting before. "I was able to find some food. These sandwiches are from the vending machine. It was all they had, along with chips and a cola." He handed Jess a sandwich, a bag of chips and a drink.

"Thanks," Jess said as she took the food from Detective Armstrong and began eating.

Suddenly a knock came at the door, before it slowly opened.

"Hi, I'm nurse Jackie, you must be Jess and you are?" The nurse asked as she shook Jess's hand and then Detective Armstrong's.

"I'm Detective Armstrong, a friend of

the family," he said as he shook the nurse's hand.

All kinds of things started going through Jess's head. Was her mom ok? Why hasn't the doctor stopped by.

"Is my mom ok? We were told the doctor was going to come talk to us," Jess stated.

"I do apologize. Doctor Farahn had an emergency to attend to, but I do have great news," the nurse said with joy. "Your mom is now in her room and she's awake."

Jess looked at Detective Armstrong and smiled. "That's great news!" she said with excitement.

"Yes, it is, and I'm here to take you to her," said nurse Jackie as she led them to the elevator.

The ride was quiet. Jess checked her phone; the battery was low. She saw a message from Grayson, saying he needed to talk to her and that it was important. Right now, the only thing that she wanted to hear was how her mom was doing. She dropped her phone in her purse and rested her head against the back of the elevator and closed her eyes.

The elevator doors open. "Right this way," the nurse instructed. After a few steps they were knocking on a door, then they entered. "Ms. Vanderbilt, you have visitors." The nurse whispers as she turns to Jess and Detective Armstrong. "I will leave you all now. If you need anything, just let me know."

"Thank you," Detective Armstrong and Jess both replied.

As soon as the door closed Jess ran to her mom's bedside. "Mom...mom, are you ok?" Jess cried as she looked at her mom.

Claire slowly opened her eyes and looked at her daughter. "Jess," she whispered softly. "You're here. How did you know I was here?"

"Officer Bradley, he came to the house. He and Grayson brought me here," said Jess. "I was so worried mom. He told me you were hurt really bad and that you may not make it through the night."

Claire thought that was strange. Why would he say that? "No, no, I'm ok. Just a few bruises and some stitches and a broken arm," she said as she looked down at her left arm. "I'm lucky to be alive, but far from dead," she says with a smile as she looks over at Detective Armstrong. "Daniel."

"Claire," Detective Armstrong replied.

"What are you doing here?" Claire asked.

"As soon as I heard, I came to make sure you were ok. Tell me…" Detective Armstrong said as he came closer. "What happened?"

"You're here to investigate?" Jess questioned. "What happen to making sure she was ok?"

"Jess it's ok……he's right, something did happen. Someone ran me off the road," she said as she looked away.

"Another set of tire tracks were found. Do you know who could have done this to you?" he asked.

"No, but I know one thing, I saw someone in the road. I tried to dodge them, but when my car got rammed in the back, I lost control," Claire said as she tried to recall as much as she could from the night.

Jess didn't say much. She knew it was Sarah. What was it she was trying to tell them? She needed to find out.

"I promise we will find whoever did this to you." said Detective Armstrong.

Jess looked down at her phone. Another text from Grayson.

"Jess sweetie you need to get some rest. You have school," said Claire.

"Mom, I'm staying here with you," Jess argued.

"Daniel, can you make sure Jess gets home safe?"

"No mom, you need me here," said Jess.

"Jess I'm ok. Just go to school and take care of the house for me. I should be home soon," said Claire.

"Ok."

"Thanks sweetie," she said as she held her daughter's hand.

Jess leaned down and kissed her mother on her forehead before leaving out.

"Well, I will get Jess home. Get some rest Claire and I mean what I said. We will find out who did this to you," Detective Armstrong said as he stared Claire in her eyes.

Just as he was about to leave Claire grabbed his hand.

"Daniel, I stopped by to see Peggy Woolrich. Strange things have been happening and I went there looking for some answers," Claire whispered. "I need you to make sure Jess is safe."

Detective Armstrong shook his head in agreeance. "Will do," he said.

"Promise me you won't let anything happen to her," said Claire.

"I promise. You have my word," he stated.

"Thank you," she said as Detective Armstrong then turned and left. Claire closed her eyes and hoped that she would be released soon. She needed to be home with her daughter. Until she finds out what is going on, her daughter could be in danger and she needed to know why.

CHAPTER THIRTEEN

Detective Armstrong dropped Jess off at home and decided to wait outside in the driveway, while she got ready for school. She quickly showered and headed out the door.

"What are you still doing here?" Jess asked as she walked up to Detective Armstrong's car.

"I thought that you could use a ride," he said.

"No, I'm good," said Jess as she began walking off.

After waiting several minutes, Detective Armstrong put his car in reverse and drove off. He caught up to Jess and rolled down the passenger window.

"Are you sure you don't want a ride?"

"Yes, I'm fine," Jess said as she continued walking. "Don't you have something better to do like maybe chasing criminals, eating donuts or something?"

"Well, I'm still investigating what happened back at your house the other day and I already have my donuts," he said as he held up a white bag reading Judy's Donut Shop. "And as far as something else...I promised your mom that I would make sure you are safe. I am a man of my word."

She stops and walks towards Detective Armstrong's car. "Look I'm ok."

He didn't believe that one bit. He could see the fear in her eyes. He's been doing his job way too long to know when something was wrong and to know when someone was lying.

"Ok... maybe I'm not ok, but I will be ok. I can manage. I'm not a little kid anymore."

"No one is treating you like a kid Jess. Your mother is just trying to protect you."

Jess stared Detective Armstrong in the eyes, "I'm not the one that needs protecting."

"You care to tell me who needs

protecting?" he asked.

Jess wanted to say something. She wanted to tell him about her dreams. Maybe he could help, but she wasn't sure if he would even believe her. So, she stood there contemplating, yet she said nothing.

"Jess, here… take my card. If you need any help or when you feel like telling me what's really going on…...call me."

"Why are you being nice to me?" Jess questioned as she took Detective Armstrong's business card. It felt like déjà vu all over again, except this time it was her accepting a card from a man she despises. Mainly because she felt that he was now the reason why her mom wanted to return to her hometown.

"Well…for starters I have no reason not to. Plus, I made a promise to your mom and I intend to stick by my word."

She glanced at the card, then back at him. She must remember that he's not the enemy here. Someone else is and she plans on finding out who before it's too late.

"Well…thanks. I really need to go before I'm late," she said before walking out of sight.

Detective Armstrong sat there for a minute before deciding to follow her, but when he got around the corner she was already gone.

"A fast walker," he thought to himself. Then he drove off in the opposite direction.

Jess stood behind a large tree, waiting for Detective Armstrong to leave the area. She peeked from behind the tree. There was no sign of him, so she decided to leave to get a head start on today's mission.

Jess traced her steps back towards her house, except she didn't go home. Instead she made her way to the house across from hers. She looked around before walking up the driveway and began knocking on the front door. After the first knock, the door opened.

Jess stood there, gripping her purse that crossed her body. She paused and prepared herself for whatever may come of this visit.

"Hello Jenna?"

"What are you doing here," Jenna

asked with a look that let Jess know that she was not welcome there at all.

"Jenna I really need to talk to you. It's about Sarah."

Saying Sarah's name quickly changed Jenna's persona.

"What about Sarah?" she asked.

"A lot of weird stuff has been happening. I think Sarah is trying to tell me something. I don't know what it is. Maybe you can help shine some light on this," Jess stated.

"I don't have anything to say," Jenna said as she began to close the door but was blocked when Jess stuck her foot in the doorway.

"People are going to die. My mom is already in the hospital now because of what's going on. So please, I need your help!"

Jenna didn't bother to say anything. She was in a split decision of doing the right thing and not giving a damn. She also knew that she couldn't just stand by and watch innocent people die, but the not so innocent...she could care less.

"Fine, just for a few minutes," Jenna said as she let Jess in and pointed to the white leather sofa. "You can have a seat."

"Thanks,' Jess said as she looked around. "It's just you and your mom?"

"Yeah."

"What about your father?"

"My mom said he died when I was young."

"I'm...I'm sorry for your loss."

"How did you know I was home?" Jenna said as she sat across from Jess.

"Well...I usually see you when you leave out the door, but this time I didn't see you. Was it because of Sarah?"

She stared Jess down at the thought of saying Sarah's name out loud. Her name penetrated her thoughts and jogged her memories.

"Saturday will be a year since Sarah went missing. She was my best friend. I still miss her."

"What happened to her?"

"Why are you here?"

"I'm here to find out what happen to her."

"I don't know what happened. I wasn't even invited. I just showed up after finding out that she would even consider hanging out with those people. They're not even her type. They are bullies that only care about themselves. I don't know what why she wanted to hang out with them anyway."

"Who are they?"

Jenna looked at Jess with a rage and repeated the question. "Who are they? Seriously? You don't know who they are, when you hang out with them every day?"

"My friends?"

"Yeah, where did you think the party took place? At the church?" she laughed. Even though this wasn't a laughing matter.

"That can't be right. Grayson told me that he didn't know her. He said he's only seen her around."

"If you believe that, you are even more

gullible than I thought you were. They're not your friends. Hopefully you won't find out the hard way like Sarah."

Jess sat with her head down, wondering if Jenna was telling the truth. Did Grayson really know Sarah? If so, what is he hiding? None of this was adding up.

"Do you ever have dreams of Sarah?"

"Yeah, I miss her," said Jenna.

"No, I mean really dream of her... because I do. Sometimes, I see her in my dreams," said Jess as she stood up and began pacing the floor. "It's like... she's trying to tell me something, but she never gets a chance to. It's like something is stopping her or I always end up waking up."

Jenna noticed the necklace Jess was wearing. "No, I don't have those kinds of dreams," she said as she then too stood up. "I think you should leave."

Jenna grabbed Jess's purse and phone and forced them into her hands.

"Why, what's wrong?" Jess asked.

"You just need to leave now!" She yells.

"Jenna what's wrong? Did I do something wrong? Was it something I said?" Jess questioned.

Jess didn't know what was wrong, but she could sense that something wasn't right.

"Jenna what's wrong? You are seriously freaking me out," Jess began backing up towards the door when she heard footsteps. She didn't know which direction they were coming from, but she heard them.

"She's coming," said Jenna as the tears began forming in her eyes. "I was there. I saw everything and yet I did nothing and now...she's coming for me," she cried.

"What? What are you talking about? Who's coming? Sarah?"

"Just leave! Get out!" she yells before running upstairs, leaving Jess standing at the front door.

Before Jess could get a word out, a piercing scream coming from upstairs filled the air.

"Jenna!" she calls out, but no answer.

She slowly walks up the stairs in the direction that Jenna went. A door slightly ajar caught her attention. Was this Jenna's room? She should just leave or call for help, but she wasn't for sure who she could trust. Seems like everyone has secrets.

"Jenna are you ok? Please say something," she whispers as she places her hand on the doorknob and carefully opens it. She gasps at the sight of Jenna falling to her hands and knees.

With tears in her eyes she reached out to Jess. "Help me," she cried as blood trickled down the side of her mouth. She then fell face down revealing an ax embedded into her back.

Jess stood there screaming, body paralyzed from what she just witnessed. "Oh God!" she said as she forced her hands over her mouth, praying no one heard her scream.

She needed to leave now. She turns to leave out of the bedroom but was stopped by the sound of the front door opening.

"Oh my gosh! Oh my gosh" Jess cried repeatedly as she began to panic. She then looked for a way to escape. Her eyes immediately went to the opened window. She could hear the footsteps coming up the stairs. She threw her phone inside of her purse and draped the straps across her body, leaving her hands free as she walked quickly and quietly towards the window.

The footsteps were getting closer and closer. She looked back at Jenna, whose body was now laying in a pool of blood. It was now or never. She needed to jump, she needed to jump now!

Twelve feet from the window, she landed on her hands and knees. Twisting her right ankle in the process. She crawled to the side of the house, trying not to be seen. What did she just get herself into? She didn't bother to go home. Afraid of if she had been seen or not. She winced in pain and ran as fast as she could with nowhere in mind. She just needed to get away from the house and wrapped her mind around what is going on.

She looked down at her phone. There were several missed calls and text from her friends. Telling her to meet them at Grayson's house. "What else could go wrong?" she thought to herself. She needed to tell someone, but who could she tell. Who could she trust?

CHAPTER FOURTEEN

Jess knocked and then rang the doorbell. "Open up!" she called out as she watched over her shoulder. The door opened, and Jess rushed in past Grayson. Trying to mask the sprain in her right ankle. "You're not going to believe what happened. I just came from…" she began to say but couldn't help notice the silence in the room.

Jess looked around. Grayson, Desmond, Becca and Meghan were all there. Standing there staring at her. They've been crying. Everyone was there. Everyone except for Alaina.

"What's going on?" Jess asked.

She had an idea but wanted confirmation of what she now feared. No one said a word, but then Grayson spoke.

"It's Alaina. She's…she's," Grayson began to say but stumbled on his words.

"She's dead," said Becca.

"What do you mean she's dead?"

"Her mom, she found her this morning...in a pool of blood. They think she committed suicide." Becca cried.

Even though Jess and Alaina never got along, death is one thing she would never wish upon anyone. Not even on her worst enemy.

"Where have you been? We've been calling you," Meghan said as she walked towards Jess and looked at her suspiciously.

"What? You think I would do something crazy like that?"

"Well you never liked her," Meghan argued. You wanted her dead. You even said it! We all know Alaina would never kill herself."

"I didn't like her because she didn't like me!" Jess yelled. "Look...as much as I hated her, I never wanted her dead."

"Then where were you?" Meghan asked.

"She was with me," said Grayson.

Everyone turned and looked at him.

As if they knew exactly what went on, but they had no idea.

"Grayson and his dad drove me to the hospital last night. My mom was in a car accident. Someone tried to run her off the road."

"It's true," Grayson said as he came to stand beside Jess. "After you guys left, a few minutes later my dad showed up. We dropped her off at the hospital and then we left."

"I was there all night until this morning," said Jess.

"What about Todd? He walked her home," said Meghan. "He had been drinking. We all know how he can be whenever he drinks. He could have done it. What if he followed her home and…"

"Guys stop!" Desmond yelled. "We can't keep blaming each other. For all we know, it could have been some crazy person who followed her home and broke in."

"He's right," Becca agreed. "We all know how paranoid Alaina has been since…"

"Since Sarah disappeared," said Jess.

"Look guys...there's something I need to tell you. Something I feel you all should know."

Everyone looked at each other. Wondering what Jess had to say.

"I knew it, I knew she was lying," Meghan said as she looked at Jess.

Jess looked at Meghan and rolled her eyes. "I'm not lying. Anyway, this morning I went to see Jenna."

"Jenna, the crazy Jenna? Well, what about her?" Becca asked.

Jess could tell that they were nervous as if they were hiding something.

"Something happened. One minute I was sitting there talking to her and the next minute...she was hysterical."

"Hysterical how?" Grayson asked.

"It was like she was afraid of someone or something. She kept yelling for me to get out and I was about to, until I...until I heard her scream. When I got upstairs..."

"Wait...you went upstairs? Why didn't you just call the police?" Desmond questioned.

"When I got upstairs she had an ax in her back. There was no break in or forced entry. Do you really think they would have believed me?" Jess cried. "I heard someone come in."

"Who was it?" Becca asked. "Maybe it was the same person that killed Alaina."

"I don't know. I didn't stay around to find out. I jumped out of the window."

Grayson looked down at Jess's foot. "That explains the limp you tried to hide when you came in. So, did Jenna say anything about that night?"

"No. She never got a chance to. She only said... she's coming."

"Who's coming?" Grayson asked.

"I don't know. She just kept saying it over and over. I was scared, I...I didn't know what to do."

"Has anyone heard from Todd?" Meghan asked.

"Yeah, he should've been here by now," Becca implied. "You did text him too right?"

"Yeah, yeah. I text everyone at the same time. Just give him a minute. He probably has a hangover."

"Or he could be burning the evidence that he used to kill Alaina," said Meghan as she flopped down on the couch.

Everyone had been standing around talking, too nervous to sit down and too scared to relax. Afraid that their past has come back to haunt them. Grayson was next to take a seat, followed by the rest. Suddenly a knock came at the door.

"That should be him," said Grayson as he hurried to open the door.

Grayson peeped out of the window before opening the door. So much has been happening, he needed to make sure he wasn't opening the door for death.

"Grayson dude, what's the emergency. I got here quickly as possible," Todd stated as he came in.

"Seriously Todd? You got here as quickly as possible?"

"Yeah, what's the big deal?" Todd asked.

"Dude, I texted you almost an hour ago," said Grayson.

"Dang dude, I'm sorry. In my mind I was moving fast, but my body couldn't keep up. So, what's the emergency?"

"Someone killed Alaina last night," Meghan blurted out as she stared at Todd and everyone else.

Todd looked around at everyone staring at him. Staring at him as if he was a killer. "What do you mean she was killed?" he asked.

"It means exactly what it means!" Meghan yelled as she moved closer to Todd but was stopped when Becca grabbed her right hand. "It means she's dead and you were the last one with her!"

"What?" You think I did this to her?" he laughed.

"You think this is funny?" said Desmond as he got up from the couch.

"No, what I think is funny is the fact that my best friends are sitting here calling me a murderer!" Todd yells as he looks at his friends in disbelief. "I loved her ok, I would never do that to her."

"Sorry, I didn't know," said Meghan. "I just assume…"

"Assumed that I killed her," Todd replied. "I didn't even walk her home. I tried to be discreet like you asked Grayson, but she caught me. She told me not to follow her."

"Did you?" Grayson asked.

"No," Todd said as he looked at everyone. "Guys I swear, I didn't follow her home."

"Did you see anyone follow her?" Becca asked.

"No. I didn't see anyone, but she was acting strange."

"Strange? Strange how?" Jess asked as she moved closer to where everyone else stood.

"She was acting like someone was watching her. It creeped me out. Eventually she took off."

"Did she say anything at all? Other than not to follow her?" Grayson asked.

Todd closed his eyes to jog his memory and reopened them filled with tears. "Oh God, I didn't believe her. I should have believed her," he cried as he held his head down in his hands.

"What?" they all said in unison.

"Todd," Jess said as she came closer to stand in front of him. "What did she say?"

Todd raised his head up from the palms of his hands and looked Jess in the eyes.

"She's coming," he replied.

Jess looked at Grayson, who then held his head down. Unable to look at Jess. Unable to show the fear in his eyes. Grayson left Todd's side and had a seat on the couch. For a few seconds he sat in silence.

"Well, she didn't say who was coming. Just like Jenna," Grayson implied as he looked at Jess who was now sitting quietly.

"Sarah," Todd whispered. "She said Sarah was coming and that she wanted revenge."

Meghan began to panic. Someone needed to calm her before she started losing it.

"Meghan just calm down," Becca said as she hugged her. "We don't know if what he's saying is true. I mean really...he was drunk. He could be making this up."

"What? After all I said, you still think I'm making this up!" said Todd as he walks up to Becca and pushed her.

"Don't fucking touch her!" Desmond yells as he pushed Todd back against the wall.

"Hey! You two stop!" Grayson yells. "Everyone just chill out, ok? This isn't the time to be fighting with each other."

Desmond released his grip on Todd. "Sorry dude," he said.

"No problem," Todd replied as he held out his hand. "Friends?"

Desmond grabbed his hand and pulled him in for a hug. "Friends."

"What happen to bros before hoes?" Todd said jokingly.

"Excuse me?" Becca interrupted.

"Dude don't start," said Desmond.

"Hey, I'm joking ok. Geez everyone is so uptight."

"This isn't a time to be joking," said Grayson. "I think we should continue with our day. If we don't show up for school, it will make us look suspicious."

"I thought you said you didn't know Sarah," Jess said to Grayson.

"I never said I didn't know her. I just said I didn't know her well."

Jess couldn't help but to smile and shake her head. What else was he lying about? What else were they all lying about? It seemed like everyone was lying for each other.

"I need to get going guys." Desmond said as he got up from where he was sitting.

"Where are you going?" Becca asked.

"I have a test today and I can't miss it," he replied.

Becca played the brave and tough

one, but she was nowhere near brave or tough, at least not today. "We should stay together," she said.

"Nothing is going to happen," said Grayson. "Just be sure to keep your phones on and close by. You know...just in case anything happens."

Everyone looked down at their phones, checking the battery life.

"I'm good," said Desmond. "And I'm out," he said as he turned to leave.

"Wait we're going with you," Becca said as she pointed to herself and Meghan. "We have cheerleader practice. When it's over we can all walk home together."

"Todd are you coming?" Desmond asked.

"Might as well, I'm sure I will probably get called a killer again if I don't," Todd said as he walked out of the door.

"Alright Grayson, see you later dude," said Desmond as he closed the door behind him.

Finally, they were alone. Jess had so many questions that she needed answered and the first one started with Sarah.

"When were you going to tell me that you knew Sarah? You made me believe that you didn't know her at all."

"I don't know her that well."

"Well tell me… how well do you know her?"

Jess waited for Grayson to answer, but he said nothing.

"Grayson……what happened that night at the party?"

He looks at her with a glare in his eyes and said, "Nothing happened, we partied like teenagers do. She was there, I spoke to her and that was it."

"That's not what happened, and you know it."

"Nothing happened," he said as he walks off.

"Hey!" she said as she follows him. "Where are you going?"

"I need to get my backpack. If my dad sees my stuff at home and not at school, he will flip out."

"Hope you didn't mind me coming up here with you?"

"No, it's cool," Grayson said as they entered his room. "So why are you so interested in knowing what happened anyway? She related to you?"

"Um...if I told you, you wouldn't believe me," she said.

"Try me," he smiled as he threw his books and other school supplies into his backpack.

Jess smiled back, but on the inside, she wanted nothing more than to find out what happened on the night Sarah went missing. While Grayson was busy getting his things together, she took this moment to glance around.

"You have a lot of trophies," said Jess.

"Yeah, my parents made sure to put me in every sport that they could think of," he replied from the bathroom.

One trophy stood out. A trophy that was labeled as hockey. The top part was missing, leaving just the bottom attached to the base. She grabs it from off the shelf and examines it.

"What happened to this trophy?" she asked as she turns around and sees Grayson standing there with a towel around his waist. "Oh my goodness...you never said anything about a shower."

He ignores her comments while he plugs in his cellphone. "That trophy got broken when we first moved into this house. I'm guessing one of the movers dropped it," he said then returned to the bathroom to finish getting ready.

The dream that she had of Sarah showed her face beaten and bloody as the worms crawled out of the holes scattered across her face. Jess looked over to his phone that was plugged in. He was hiding something, and she was going to find out. She unplugs it and goes through his videos. She finds nothing until she went through his photos. There she finds pictures of him and Sarah in his room, in his bed. She looks closely and sees the trophy in the background.

"When did you say you moved into this house?" she calls out.

"Two years ago," he replies.

Something didn't add up. She goes back to the videos and finds a hidden file. She clicks on it and it opens, revealing Sarah talking while Grayson held the camera. She also noticed the necklace Sarah was wearing. She pulls the necklace from out of her shirt and holds it in the palm of her hand. She turned it over, revealing initials S.J.W. engraved on it. It belongs to Sarah.

"She chose me," she whispers to herself.

"Who chose you?" Grayson asked as his voice faded at the sound of Sarah's voice followed by his, playing on the video. Then he noticed the necklace Jess was wearing. "Looks like we both have some explaining to do."

CHAPTER FIFTEEN

It was the middle of the school day. Desmond was finishing up his exams while Becca and Meghan finished up cheerleading practice in the gym.

"Hey Becca," said Meghan.

"Yeah," Becca said in between doing cheers.

"I don't want to die," she whispers.

"Wait...what?"

"I don't want to die," Meghan said as she began to cry.

"Hey," Becca said as she pulled Meghan aside to a corner, so that no one could hear them. "Don't say that. You're not going to die. Whoever is doing this is just trying to scare us into talking."

"Maybe we should talk," she stated.

"No!" Becca yelled, but quickly

lowered her voice. "Do you know what could happen if we say something?"

"We didn't do anything wrong," Meghan sobbed.

"Then I guess we don't have anything to worry about." Becca said with a reassuring smile. "Let's just stick together and watch each other's back."

"Ok," said Meghan.

"How about we go shower and skip the rest of the day?" said Becca.

"Sounds good. Just don't leave me alone."

"Don't worry I won't," Becca said as she forced another smile as they headed towards the girls' locker room. She was more than scared, she was terrified. Her heart raced from just the thought of dying. How did it feel? Will there be pain? Questions she hopes she wouldn't have to find out. At least no time soon.

"So, when were you going to tell me about you and Desmond?" Meghan asked as she and Becca headed towards the lockers.

"There's no us...we're just friends,"

she lied.

"Oh really," Meghan replied.

"Yes really," Becca said as she shoved her things in the locker and hastily walked to the showers. She tried to avoid the conversation, but Meghan was right behind her.

"Becca...we've been friends since kindergarten. You can tell me, I promise I won't tell anyone," Meghan said as they got ready to get in the shower stall.

She was in one while Becca was in another one. She tried her best to avoid talking about her relationship with Desmond for the sake of their friendship. She knew Meghan had a crush on him.

"Becca are you even listening to me? Becca said nothing. "Hello?... Earth to Becca?"

"Yeah, I'm listening," she replied.

"So, how long have you two been dating?" she asked again.

"We've just started," she said.

"Just started like in two days ago or

just started like a few weeks ago?"

She hesitated at first, but she knew that if she didn't say something now, Meghan would keep pestering her until she did. "More like a few months ago," she stated.

"Oh wow," Meghan replied. Becca could hear the disappointment in Meghan's voice. Therefore, she didn't want to say anything right away. "You know you could have told me. I thought I was supposed to be your best friend. I tell you everything."

"Meghan, I didn't want you to get upset."

"Get upset. Should I be upset that my best friend that's consoling me is dating someone that I have a crush on? It was supposed to be me and him."

"See, this is exactly why I didn't want to tell you. I knew you would get upset."

"I'm not upset."

"Yes, you are."

"No, I'm not. I'm disappointed. I just didn't expect this from my best friend," Meghan said as she turns off the shower and left.

Becca continued showering. She didn't bother to go after her. She wanted to give her time to calm down. They have arguments all the time, this time was no different.

"Meghan I'm sorry ok. Let's not end our friendship over some guy. I love you, you're my bestie!" she yells.

She became silent after hearing footsteps coming close.

"I knew you would come back. Meghan?" she said as the shower beside her turns on. A sense of relief instantly calms her nerves. "Meghan please talk to me," she calls out, but still no answer.

She knew Meghan would be mad at her, but usually they get over things quick. Maybe, just maybe this time she overstepped the friend zone.

"Meghan please say something. I'm really sorry."

She was getting nowhere. Meghan wasn't talking to her now. No matter how hard she tried. Then suddenly she heard a small sob coming from the shower next to her.

"Meghan I'm sorry."

She never meant to make her cry. The cry became louder and louder causing Becca to turn the water down, giving Meghan her undivided attention so she wouldn't lose her as a friend.

"Please don't cry," said Becca.

"You hurt me," she cries.

"I...I never meant to hurt you Meghan."

"I thought you wanted to be friends," she cries again.

"We are friends, no one will come between us, I promise."

"Then why did you hurt me?"

Becca turned the water off and grabbed a towel. "I didn't mean to hurt you. Can we talk about this later?"

"She's coming."

"Who's coming?" Becca asked. "Meg are you ok. You sound weird."

"You will die. You will all die."

"Meghan…I'm…what did you say?" Becca asked as she pulled her towel tight around her body and yanked open the shower curtain. She slowly walks out of her shower and stands in front of the shower next to her. "Meghan," she calls out as she placed her hand on the curtain, but there was no answer. "Meghan," she calls out again.

"Who are you talking to?" Meghan questioned as she stood in the doorway. "Your boyfriend is waiting on you."

Becca turned towards Meghan with an uneasy look in her eyes. "I…I was just talking to you."

"Um…excuse me, but I'm standing right here," Meghan said as she looked down at her phone. She received a text message from an unidentified number. She suddenly looked back up at Becca with a frightened look on her face.

"If it wasn't you…" she began to say as her eyes filled with tears. "Then it's her. It's her, isn't it?" she asked as the tears slid down her face.

Meghan couldn't say a word, she just shook her head yes. She then held up her phone showing Becca the text message she had just received, "SHE'S COMING" it read.

"She's behind me, isn't she?" Becca cried.

Meghan once again shook her head yes and cried.

"I'm sorry Meghan. I'm so... sorry," said Becca.

Meghan screamed as she watched her friend's throat being sliced opened from ear to ear. She wanted to run to her, but it was too late. Becca's lifeless body fell onto the hard floor as the blood squirted from her neck, painting the floor red.

Meghan took off running in disbelief in what she just saw. Her best friend murdered by a dead girl. A girl that she helped murder. She ran and ran until she bumped into Desmond.

"Hey slow down. I thought I heard someone scream."

"Desmond," Meghan cried hysterically. "It's Becca. We need to call the police. We need to get help."

"Hold up what's going on?" he asked.

"It's Becca, she's dead."

"Wait what? What do you mean she's dead?" he asked as he looked past her.

"She's dead. We need to go. We need to go now!"

"She can't be dead," he said.

"Desmond, she's dead. We need to go get help."

Desmond didn't bother to listen to Meghan. He needed to see for himself. "I need to see her," he said as he took off and ran past Meghan.

"Desmond!" she yells, but he still wasn't listening. She wanted to run out of there as fast as she could, but she was too scared to leave out of there alone. "Desmond!" she yells again, this time running after him. She ran until she stumbled across him, kneeling beside her best friend's body. She needed to be strong. "We really should leave. We don't know if the killer is still in here."

"We can't just leave her here." He looks up at her with tears in his eyes. "I was supposed to protect her." He looks around the room with vengeance now in his heart and yells, "Where are you, you coward!"

"Desmond we really need to get help and find the others."

"Ok," he said as he raised up from where he was kneeling and wiped his face. His heart has never been as cold as it was right now. Someone will pay for what they did to Becca. "Let's go."

They both took one last look at Becca's body as it laid lifeless on the floor, before running to go get help.

Minutes later the school was surrounded by police. Blue lights filled the air while students and the faculty were being escorted to a safe area. All eyes were on Meghan and Desmond, since they were the last ones to see Becca alive. You could hear the whispers of rumors being speculated amongst the crowd.

"I don't like this," Meghan whispered. "Everyone is staring at us like we are murderers. We didn't do anything."

"Don't worry about it. We've already talked to the cops. Who cares what other's think?"

"I care. It's my fault," she said.

"What are you talking about?"

"Becca and I were supposed to stay together. We had an argument and I left. If I would have stayed, this wouldn't have happened."

"It's not your fault. If you would have stayed, if could have been both of you. So, don't beat yourself up over it," Desmond stated.

"I shouldn't have left her. I can't help but to feel like I killed her. I should have stayed with her," Meghan said with regrets.

"You didn't kill her. From now on we need to stick together. The killer is somewhere out there. Whoever it is knows about what happened that night and they're picking us off one by one."

CHAPTER SIXTEEN

Jess ran home as fast as she could and locked herself inside. There she stood, breathing heavily as she rested her back against the door.

"Jess open the door," Grayson demanded as he knocked on the door.

"Go away!" she yelled.

"We need to talk."

"Go away Grayson. I have nothing to say to you. You practically lied. You lied about everything.

"I didn't lie. Ok...I lied about some things, but I did not kill Sarah," he whispered as he looked around, making sure no one else was there.

"I don't believe you!"

"I swear. It's the truth. You have to believe me."

Jess remained silent. She didn't know what to do. She still didn't trust Grayson, yet she needed his help.

"Jess please," he begged just as his phone rang.

Jess couldn't hear the conversation, but she could tell by the sound of his voice that something was wrong.

"That was Desmond. Becca is dead," he said.

This could be a trick to try to get inside and she wasn't falling for it, or was she?

"How do I know that?"

"Check your phone, Meghan tried calling you. They're on their way over."

She reached into her back pocket for her phone and saw the messages, including a voicemail from Meghan.

"Gosh," she said to herself. What if Grayson was still lying? What if they were all in on it? All these questions of what ifs were forming in her mind. She trusted her gut and opened the door.

"Thank you," he said as he walked in.

"Don't try anything," she stated.

"I'm not and I'm not planning to," he replied.

"Then why did you run after me?"

"Because it wasn't what it seems?"

"Which part? The broken trophy or the I don't know her story?"

"What about you?" he asked.

"What about me?" she questioned with a stare. "I have nothing to do with any of this and somehow I'm caught up in this nonsense. I never wanted to come here. I miss my old friends."

"I'm sorry," Grayson replied.

Jess was beginning to feel sympathetic. His sincerity sounded real, like he was genuinely sorry for lying.

"So tell me, how did you get Sarah's necklace?" he asked.

"My mom bought it for me the same day we arrive in town," she replied. "So tell me, what happened that night at the party?"

said Jess as she stared Grayson directly in the eyes. Showing him that she wasn't afraid of him and she wasn't backing down. She wanted answers and she wanted them now. "I'm waiting."

"Jess, she was at the party and I ran into her and we talked."

"What happened to her? People are dying because of what happened."

"We don't know that."

"Yes, we do. Ever since I've arrived here, I've seen Sarah in my dreams. Sometimes it feels like she's trying to tell me something. She wants revenge Grayson, so yeah excuse me for trying to figure this out. So, tell me what the hell happened!?" she yelled.

Grayson began pacing the floor as he then replayed that night in his mind over.

"It wasn't supposed to end up this way…I swear," he said as he quickly wiped a tear away. He avoided eye contact as much as possible. He didn't want Jess to see him as weak. "We were playing truth or dare."

"Let me guess…you chose dare?"

Grayson nodded yes as he finally stopped pacing the floor and they both took a seat on the sofa.

"So, what kind of dare was it?"

"They dared me to make out with Sarah," he replied. "It happened so fast. She was getting out of control, kicking and hitting. I didn't know what to do. So, I grabbed the trophy, but I swear I didn't kill her. She was still alive when I left her there."

"All because she said no? That explains the broken trophy." Jess stated as she got up from the sofa. She couldn't stand sitting beside Grayson right now. "I really thought you were different."

"What? I didn't rape her. It was consensual. She had a few drinks and...I don't know. Everything happened so fast Jess. What was I supposed to do? I'm the star player on the football team. I couldn't go down like a punk."

"Oh my goodness! Do you hear yourself? You're nothing but a self-centered prick."

"Look, I never meant for any of this to

happen, but I couldn't risk her going to the police. It would have ruined my name and scholarship."

"Sure, poor old Grayson. Who all was in on this?" she asked.

"Me, Desmond, Meghan, Jeffrey and the others," he replied.

"Wait, if whoever is behind this is killing everyone that was involved, why did they kill Sarah's friend Jenna?"

"Jenna was there. She walked in on me with Sarah. Sarah called out for her, but she just left. That's all I know," Grayson replied just as the doorbell rang. "It's probably Desmond and Meghan."

Jess hurried to the door. As soon as she opened it, Meghan and Desmond rushed in. They were a mess mentally. Meghan was paranoid constantly looking out the window and looking over her shoulders. While Desmond was covered in blood.

"Meghan just calm down," Jess insisted.

"Calm down? You want me to calm down after watching my friend get murdered! Meghan yelled. "We need to go to the police and tell them what happened that night."

"Hey, don't say that out loud," said Desmond as he stood in front of Meghan.

"It's ok guys...Jess knows," said Grayson as he looked at Meghan and Desmond. They looked at each other before looking at Jess.

"What do you mean she knows?" Desmond questioned.

"She knows. I told her everything."

"We need to go to the police! I don't want to die. We're all going to die!" Meghan yelled.

"We're not going to die! Stop saying that!" Desmond yelled back.

"She's right ok! As much as I want to admit it, but she's right. We're all going to die. We need to figure out something fast," said Grayson.

"So, where do we start?" Desmond asked.

"I don't know?" Grayson replied.

"How about starting with that night of the party. Who all was there and who would benefit from this?" Jess stated.

"All of us was there and a few kids from school. It was all that my dad would allow. He said he didn't want to spend his off day babysitting a bunch of drunk teenagers," said Grayson.

"What? Wait a minute. Your dad was there?" Jess asked.

"Yeah," said Grayson as he looked down at his hands. "My dad was later charged with providing alcohol to a minor, times ten."

"Your dad can't run for mayor with charges like that."

"I know, that's why he hired the best attorney in the state. Got all charges dismissed," he stated.

"We need to get in contact with your dad, he could be in danger," Jess insisted.

"He should be at one of the precincts, he's filling in for a buddy of his. He has more than enough protection there."

"Ok great. What about the attorney

that got your dad's charges dismissed. Do you know his name, maybe we can track him down?" Jess stated.

"Um I think his name is... Frank Vanderbilt," Grayson said slowly as he looked at Jess. He already knew what she was thinking.

"No, tell me you're wrong. That can't be right," she cried. "Frank Vanderbilt is my dad. That's why she chose me. She chose me because of my dad."

"Jess I'm sorry," Grayson said.

"Yeah you are. You all are, because of your stupid decision, innocent people are going to die!" she yells.

"Enough already!" Meghan screamed through tears. "I'm tired of sitting here listening to you play the blame game. We made a mistake ok, we get it. I just lost two of my best friends and I don't want to lose anymore."

Desmond gathered Meghan in his arms and hugged her. "We're all going to be ok," he said. Those words were all she wanted to hear right now.

Everyone became quiet as they remained seated. Each trying to make sense of everything and hoping they weren't next to die. After several minutes, Meghan was the first to break the silence.

"I saw her," she said.

"You saw who?" Jess asked.

"I left out of the shower room, but I came back because I heard Becca talking. I received a message on my phone and when I looked up, that's when I saw her...Sarah."

"How do you know it was her?" said Grayson.

"I just know," she replied. "she looked me in the eyes as she took an ax or hatchet or whatever it was and..." Meghan couldn't finish her words. Replaying that gruesome scene in her mind was just too much for her to handle.

"Wait, Jess remember the ax we saw in your basement?" Grayson asked.

"Yeah, the old disgusting ax, what about it?" she replied.

"That day when we were down in the basement, the ax was there."

"Ok what are you getting at?"

"It was gone when Desmond, Todd and I went down there later."

"What? How is that possible?"

"I don't know, but you know what that means."

"The killer has been in this house," said Jess.

"It also means that, we know who's doing the killing," Desmond said as they all looked at him.

CHAPTER SEVENTEEN

Jess's mom Claire laid in bed as the electric vital monitor beeped continuously. The doctor had previously visited her, informing her that she could go home tomorrow. This was great news but leaving today would have been better.   All day her mind has been on her daughter and her conversation with Peggy. She needed to get home today. Something didn't feel right. Claire grabbed her cellphone from off the table beside her. She needed to make sure her daughter was ok. She began dialing her daughter's number just as a knock came at the door.

"It's open," she called out right as her daughter answered her phone.

"Mom," she said surprisingly.

"Are you at school?" Claire asked. "Who is that in the background?"

"It's just my friends.," Jess said nervously. She knew her mom would be upset about her missing school, but she didn't want to lie about it. "Mom...I didn't go to school today, but I have a really good explanation."

"This had better be good young lady. You know you're not supposed to skip school. Your father and I paid good money for you to go to the best school Jess."

"Mom I know," she replied. "But..."

"But nothing. You can't skip school Jess. What am I going to do with you?"

"Mom you don't understand. I've been..."

"Jess I have to go. Officer Bradley just stopped by and I don't want to be rude by being on the phone. We will talk about this later young lady when I get home."

"What? Mom wait!" she yells. "Officer Bradley helped kill Sarah!" she yells again but was too late. Her mom had already ended the call.

"I'm sorry about that. That was my daughter. Apparently, she skipped school today," Claire said with a friendly smile.

Officer Bradley smiled as he came

closer to her bed. "I have one of my own, so I know what you mean," he said. "I remember when Grayson skipped school last year. I grounded him for two weeks."

"So, um…what brings you by today? I know it couldn't be the food," she laughed.

He smiled. "Just stopping by to see how you were doing? I saw your car, you're lucky to be alive."

"Yeah, that's what I was told. I don't remember too much. When I woke up I was in here," Claire said as her phone began ringing. She looked down and noticed it was her daughter calling her back. She hit the ignore button. Within a few seconds her phone rang again and again. She was too upset to talk right now. More like disappointed.

"You need me to come back another time?" he asked.

"No, it's ok. It's just my daughter again. Probably begging for me not to ground her. She wanted me to not treat her like a child and when I decided to, she skipped school."

"Kids," Officer Bradley stated.

Claire's phone sounded again. She was getting impatient right about now. She didn't want to hear any excuses coming from Jess's mouth. Until she saw a text message.

Jess: Mom officer Bradley help kill Sarah! Stay away from him mom!

Claire slowly looked up at Officer Bradley who was smiling down at her.

"Everything's ok?" he asked.

"Yeah, everything's ok," she replied nervously.

"You sure? You look like you seen a ghost."

"I'm ok," Claire said as she threw the covers off her and placed both feet on the ground. "I think I'm going to go get some air."

Officer Bradley came closer as he reached behind his back and pulled out a gun.

"Well, it seems like your daughter has been doing her homework," he said with a laugh as he began loading his gun.

"I guess so," she replied.

"I wasn't planning on having two bodies in my trunk, but I think I might have enough room," he said.

"You're crazy! You can't get away with what you have done!" she yells.

"Oh, but I can, I got away once with it thanks to your husband," he said as he smiles. "Get up and get your clothes on, we're leaving."

"What? I can't just leave," she said.

He cocked his gun and placed it to Claire's forehead. "You can, and you will."

"Ok, ok. Just don't kill me," she begged.

"Quit stalling. You have three minutes, or I will shoot you right where you sit."

"You're not that crazy."

Officer Bradley pulls out a silencer and placed it at the end of his gun. "Anything else you want to say?" he asked.

"Why are you doing this?" she cried as she grabbed her pants from off the chair and began pulling them on.

Officer Bradley ignored her as he began texting someone on his phone. Claire stared at him with fear. She took a deep breath and looked around the room for a weapon. She didn't see a weapon, but she did see the button to call a nurse. She slowly moved her hand to the control device laying on the bed and grabbed it.

"What are you doing?" he asked.

"I'm just turning the tv off."

Within a few minutes a nurse came over the speaker on the control. "Yes Ms. Vanderbilt. How can I help you?"

Claire froze as she looked at Officer Bradley. She didn't know what to do. She wanted to yell for help, but Officer Bradley held a picture of her daughter Jess up on his phone. She knew then that this was a fight she had to face alone.

"Ms. Vanderbilt are you ok?" the nurse calls out.

"Um...yeah I'm ok. I must have pushed the wrong button by mistake."

"Ok, well if you need anything we're here. I'm nurse Corrine and I will be here all day ok?"

"Ok. Thank you," Claire said as she looked directly at Officer Bradley. This time, it wasn't with fear... it was with revenge. "Let's go."

They made their way out of the hospital and into his pickup truck. Claire knew right away that the pickup truck looked familiar. He tied her hands behind her back before shoving her in the passenger side of the truck.

"Oh my God, it was you. You were there that night. You ran me off the road. You tried to kill me!" she yells. "Why are you doing this?"

"You Vanderbilt's think you can just put your nose wherever you want. Things were just fine until your husband, you and your daughter decided to come along."

"What are you talking about? My daughter has nothing to do with this and so does my husband."

"When your husband took my case a while back, he also took my wife. Now you and your daughter come along and rattle the cage. Stirring up things and causing problems."

"I had no idea. I'm sorry ok. Whatever you do, please," she begged. "Please leave my daughter out of this. She's just a child."

He said nothing. He drove in silence until they were away from the hospital. He didn't want to listen to anything Claire had to say.

"Officer Bradley please, you don't have to do this. You need to turn yourself in. You have..." she began to say right before Officer Bradley took his right hand and back handed her right across her face.

She screamed from the pain. She wanted to touch her face, but her hands were tied and there was no way she could get out. Tears began forming in her eyes and slowly cascaded down her cheeks. Her eyes felt heavy. She needed to close them, but she also needed to stay awake to know where he was taking her.

"I didn't want to get involved, I had no choice. My daughter claimed she saw Sarah. I wanted to find out what exactly happened to her. That's why I visited Peggy," she stated. "Peggy. Is Peggy ok?"

Officer Bradley said nothing as he

continued driving.

"You know I hope you rot in hell. You won't get away with this!" she yells just as he grabs her head and rams it into the dashboard.

She cries as she laid her head against the door. She began closing her eyes until she was awakened by a bump in the road. She slowly opened her eyes and they widen as she looked around. She knew this place. This is where she first saw the girl.

"Where are you taking me?" she asked as the truck came to a halt. She winced from the pain in her head, causing her to lay her head back against the headrest.

He remained quiet as he put his truck into park and got out. Her eyes followed him as he went to the bed of his truck and began retrieving objects. She needed to seize the moment and run. She had a long life to live and today would not be the day of her death. Not if she had anything to do with it.

She eased her body around, so she could get a good look at him. "Oh my goodness," Claire cried as she saw the shovel, tape and other items that indicated that he was planning on murdering her.

She turned back around and began to panic. Her eyes roamed his truck, searching for anything to help cut the rope that bounded her hands together. She eased her back against the armrest and began feeling around for anything that could be useful. She searched until she felt a small pocket knife in the armrest under some papers. She didn't know if it would work, but it was all that she could find, so it had to work.

She took the knife and secured it in her hand by balling her fist tightly around it, so she wouldn't drop it. This was her last chance for survival. She looked back at Officer Bradley and he was no longer at the bed of the truck. Seeing him gone brought a smile to her face. This was her chance to make a move and run. Run as fast as she could until she reached the road.

She placed her back close to the door, so she could reach the handle. She grabbed hold of the door handle and pressed her body against the door to help push it open. The door didn't budge. She pulled and pushed and pulled again on the door handle. Still nothing. "You have to be kidding me," she cried.

She looked at the door and noticed,

there was no lock on the door. She could go crawl out of the driver side door, but it was too late. Officer Bradley was coming towards the truck from out of the woods. Her heart began to thump harder and harder the closer he got. There was only one chance left.

As soon as he opened her door, Claire took her right foot and kicked him as hard as she could between his legs, causing him to fall backwards onto the ground. She took off running as fast as she could as he laid there holding himself, wincing from the intense pain.

Claire ran because her daughter's life depended on it, but she couldn't outrun the shots that were now being fired at her. Shot after shot was fired, with one striking her in her right leg, causing her to stumble and scream from the pain.

She ran but had no idea where she was running to. The road had to be close by. She looked behind her as she ran for her life, with no sign of him trailing her. Hoping she lost him, she stopped and hid behind a big tree.

She kneeled and rested her back against it. She took the pocket knife and began cutting away at the ropes. It was too dull, but it was all that she had. She continued trying to cut and cut, until finally it penetrated the first surface, then second. She was happy and relieved.

She needed to reach her phone in her back pocket. She was just one more cut away, when the last piece of rope gave in setting her hands free. She immediately tore off a piece of her gown and applied pressure to her leg before wrapping it, hoping to stop the bleeding. She didn't have much time, she needed to get help.

She reached into her back pocket and pulled out her phone. She saw there were three missed calls from Daniel. She began dialing Daniels phone number. "Please answer," she whispers.

"This is Detective Armstrong how may I...."

"Daniel" she said with joy. "Daniel thank God you answered."

"Claire? Where the hell have you been? I've been calling you. The hospital said you had left without checking out. Are you ok? You sound out of breath."

"Daniel, I need your help. I'm in trouble. Officer Bradley is trying to kill me. He came to the hospital and held me at gun point. I'm somewhere in the woods..." she cried.

"I'm on my way. Just keep your phone on so I can track you," he said.

"Daniel hurry. I don't..." was all she could say before she was knocked out.

"Hello? Claire are you ok? Claire!" he yells as he waited for her to respond.

Officer Bradley picks up Claire's phone to see who she was talking to. He then throws the phone against the tree, breaking it into pieces.

"You won't get rescued today," he said as he throws her over his shoulder and walks off.

CHAPTER EIGHTEEN

Jess stood there looking at Grayson and the others. She still couldn't believe what they all had done, including his dad. Now they all needed to figure out how to stay alive.

"So, since we figured out the killer. What do we do now?" Jess asked as her phone rang. "That's odd, it's the hospital."

"Maybe it's your mom," said Grayson.

"No, my mom wouldn't call from the hospital unless her battery died," she said.

"Ok well maybe the battery died or maybe you should just answer it," said Desmond.

"Hello," she said as she looked at her friends. "Oh my God," she gasps. "Ok thank you."

"What's wrong?" they asked.

"Apparently, my mom is missing from the hospital. This can't be happening," she cried.

"It's possible that she could have left," said Grayson.

"I know my mom. She wouldn't just up and leave just like that. Besides, she was supposed to be discharged tomorrow. She had no reason to run away like that."

"Just face it, maybe she was next on Sarah's mom kill list," said Grayson.

"How could you say that? She's alive I just know it," she said as she came to stand in front of Grayson.

"Look, we've all lost someone, or have you forgotten?" said Grayson.

Jess thought about Grayson's sister Alaina and then Becca. "Sorry, I just can't lose my mom, she's all I have here."

"I'm sorry too. I shouldn't have said that. I think we should pay Sarah's mom a visit. We can sneak in," Grayson suggested.

"Yeah, just what we need, another murder charge along with breaking and entering," Desmond said nonchalantly. "No thank you, I'm tired of hiding."

"I can't go. I need to wait here for my mom. What if she's on her way here and needs me?" Jess stated.

"Not to ruin the moment but I think we should go to the police," Meghan stated. "I don't want to wait around for some crazy person to kill me."

"How many times do you have to say that," said Desmond. "We're not going to die."

"Yeah that's what you said before and look at what happened to Becca."

"That was before we knew who the killer was," Desmond stated.

"We're still not for sure if she's the killer or not," said Jess. "We can't just jump to conclusions without knowing all the facts."

"Well, one fact is that you stay in the same house. We need to check out your house. If she's the killer, there must be a way she's getting in," said Desmond.

They all agreed as they checked every window and door, except for Jess's room. Ever since the incident, the room was off limits. At least for her it was. She wanted no part of that room or the house. If she had it her way, she'd be back in her hometown with her old friends.

They finished their way around the house and made their way back into the living room where they sat and waited in fear.

"Why hasn't she killed me?" Jess asked as everyone looked at her. "I'm just saying. We've been living here in this house, for a few weeks now and I'm still alive. If she wanted to kill me, I'm sure she would have done it by now."

"Unless," said Grayson.

"Unless what?" Jess replied.

"Unless she's saving you for reincarnation of her daughter."

"What?" Jess laughed. "Do you know how crazy that sounds? It sounds crazy and you sound crazy for saying something like that."

"It sounds crazy, but why else would she keep you alive?" said Grayson. "Think about it. You're right here in her playground and you're still alive."

"A while back there was a rumor around school," said Desmond. "Everyone believed Sarah's mom could bring back the dead and if she hated you bad enough she could make you vanish."

"I had nothing to do with any of this and I damn sure didn't ask to be a part of this," said Jess. She began pacing the floor, trying to wrap her brain around everything and connect the dots. "I don't know what else to do other than stay alive."

"Yeah I think that's all of our options for now. Unless we go to the police," Desmond suggested.

"What? So, you're turning against me now?" Grayson said as he questioned Desmond face to face.

"Dude, I'm not turning against you," said Desmond.

"If I go down, we all go down," Grayson argued.

"Yo, technically we didn't kill her, you and your pops did," Desmond replied.

"You all were there. So, you're just as guilty," Grayson said with an attitude as he pointed to Desmond and Meghan.

"He's right," said Jess. "I don't know much about the law or the criminal justice system, but just from listening to my dad, he's right."

"Fuck! We are screwed!" Desmond yelled.

"We just need to come up with a plan," said Grayson.

"So, in the meantime we wait to get chopped up?" Desmond asked.

"In the meantime, we stay alive," Grayson suggested.

"What about Todd?" Jess asked.

"I haven't heard from him," said Grayson. "I tried calling and texting him, but no response as usual."

"You know Todd, he's never in pocket," Desmond stated.

"We need to go to his house and..." Desmond began to say.

"No way, not this again. We've talked about this. What about my mom?"

"We will go over and make sure he's ok, then come straight back," said Grayson.

Jess had to seriously think about it. She didn't want to be away just in case her mom showed up and needed her help. She also wanted to help her friends out too.

"How about Desmond and I go check on Todd, while you stay here with Jess?" Meghan asked. She only wanted to be alone with Desmond. This was another perfect time to seize the opportunity.

"No," said Jess as she looked at everyone. "We should stay together. We all know what will happen if we split up. I'll go, but we have to be quick."

"Fine," said Grayson.

"I'm serious Grayson. There is a chance my mom may be still alive."

"Yeah ok," he replied. "We'll be quick."

"Ok, well let's get going," said Desmond.

He was the first to head towards the door. The rest followed behind him, prepared and determined to find an end to everything. Their main fear was dying and losing another friend.

"What are we waiting on?" Jess asked.

"Your door is jammed," Desmond replied as he pulled on the door.

"What are you talking about? There's nothing wrong with the door." Jess stated as she joined Desmond at the door. She began pulling on the door, but it wouldn't budge. She checked the deadbolt and pulled again before giving up. "That's strange. It won't open," she said.

"Yep, that's what I just said," said Desmond.

"Let me try," said Grayson as he took his turn pulling and pulling. "Someone must have jammed the door."

"We locked all the doors and windows, how is that possible?" Meghan asked.

"It's locked from the outside Meghan, not inside," said Grayson. "Is there another way out?"

"There's the back door and...there's the basement," Jess replied.

"Ok, we can split up and meet back

here or we can stay together," said Desmond.

"We can split up," Meghan insisted again as she moved closer to Desmond.

"No, we all stay together. You're going to get us all killed. If you want to go alone go ahead," Jess said.

"I agree," said Grayson. "We should check out the back door first and then the basement."

Everyone made their way to the back door as Jess prayed silently, hoping that it would open. It was jammed as well.

"Gosh," said Jess.

"We need to check the basement. There has to be a way out," said Grayson.

Jess slowly opened the basement door. It was dark, cold and uninviting. They stood at the top of the stairs. No one made a move.

"I'll go first," Desmond said as he took the lead, showing no fear.

"The light is at the bottom of the stairs," said Jess as she followed behind

Grayson, with Meghan behind her. They each used the light on their phone to see their way.

Their hearts pounded against their chest as they took a deep breath. Soon this will all be over and for some maybe sooner.

Desmond reached the bottom of the stairs and searched for the light switch. "I still don't understand why this house doesn't have a light at the top of the stairs," he fussed as he finally came across the light switch. "The switch is not working."

"Well pull the chain that's hanging down," said Jess.

The light was dim. It didn't give off much light, but just enough to see their way around the crowded basement. Just as they reached the bottom of the stairs the light began to flicker.

"I don't like this one bit. I have a bad feeling about this." said Meghan.

"Shhh, you guys hear that?" Jess whispered.

"Hear what?" Grayson replied.

"Footsteps," said Jess.

They all stopped their movement to listen. To see if they could hear the footsteps too and they did. The footsteps were getting closer towards the basement door.

"We need to hide," Desmond whispers.

"I'm coming with you," Meghan said as she followed Desmond and Jess followed Grayson.

They all agreed as they found places to hide in the old creepy basement. They waited quietly in the dark corners.

"Hello," the voice calls out. "Hey, you guys down here, I got the text."

"Todd?" Desmond calls out.

"Who else is it supposed to be," Todd replied as they all came from hiding.

"Todd where in the fuck have you been man? We've been calling you," Grayson said with rage.

"Dude chill out. I was in detention. You know we can't have our phones in there. I checked my phone and came right over," Todd replied as he stood at the top of the stairs.

Something just didn't sit right with Jess. Was Todd in on everything too. "How did you get in?" Jess asked.

"What? What do you mean how did I get in?" Todd replied.

"The doors were locked, and all the windows were locked too. How did you get in?" Jess yelled as everyone looked at Todd.

"I came in through the front door," he said.

No one said a word. They just looked at him, then looked at each other. They didn't know what or who to believe at this point.

"Guys," Todd said as he took a step forward, causing them to take a step back. "I'm not lying," he said as the door behind him opened wider.

"Oh my God!! Todd watch out!" Meghan screams.

Todd looked around and met the gaze of a bloody ax coming down right on top of his head. The blood gushed out, running down his face. He reached up and touched his head. His brains were slightly oozing out.

He turns around facing his friends.

"See...it wasn't me," he said with tears in his eyes.

They all stood there in disbelief as they watched Todd's body tumbling down the stairs. They looked up and saw Sara's mom at the top of the stairs holding the bloody ax before closing the door.

"I think I'm going to puke," Meghan said as she ran to a nearby corner and began hurling.

Minutes later they all stood around Todd's body. They searched the basement for something to cover up his body. They couldn't stand being in the same room with a dead body.

"I smell something burning," said Desmond. "She's burning the house down!"

"There has to be another way to get out down here," said Grayson. "If there's a way in, there's a way out. We need to split up. This basement should go the full length of the house, but this one doesn't," he said curiously as he walked over to a wall and began feeling around on it."

"What are you doing?" Jess asked.

"Looking for a door," he replied. "If the basement goes the entire length of the house, that means someone closed off half of it."

"But why?" she asked.

"I don't know, but we need to find out quick. It's only a matter of time before the smoke gets in here," said Grayson. "Everyone, feel around on the wall. There has to be a door."

Everyone took their position and began doing as asked. They began removing things off the wall, tools, pictures, peg boards and old bikes, before coming across a tall wooden bookcase.

"Guys, check this out," said Desmond. They all stopped what they were doing to see what Desmond had found.

"What is it?" Grayson asked.

"I think there's something behind this. Here, help me move it," said Desmond.

Grayson got on one side while Desmond was on the other. They both tried to move it, but it wouldn't budge.

"We can help," said Jess.

"No, that won't help. It's stuck," said Desmond.

"We have to do something fast. The smoke is beginning to creep in," Jess said as she began to panic.

"Wait," said Grayson as he began removing books from all the shelves. "There's a latch." He quickly unhooked the latch that was holding the bookcase against the wall.

"How did you know that was there?" Jess asked.

"I watch a lot of movies," he said as he and Desmond began pushing the book case out of the way, revealing a semi dark room, the other half of the basement.

"What is this?" Grayson said before coughing.

Jess and the others eased their way into the once closed off room and was face with a horrendous stench. A stench so strong that they all began coughing. They placed their hands over their nose and mouth to keep from inhaling whatever it was.

"What is that smell? It smells like someone died in here." Meghan asked.

"I can't really see anything," said Jess.

Grayson searched the wall with his hand. "I think I found a light switch," he said right before flipping the switch.

"Oh my gosh," said Jess with a horrified look on her face.

"What in the world is this?" Desmond said as they stared at the wall.

CHAPTER NINETEEN

Claire laid on the ground helplessly. Her hands were now tied again behind her back, along with her feet. She slowly opened her eyes to witness Officer Bradley digging anxiously at the ground.

"What are you doing?" she asked through her groggy voice.

"I'm doing what I should have done the same day you came in town," said Officer Bradley as he continued digging.

"But why? She cried. "Why are you doing this? We had nothing to do with any of this. Just let me go please. I won't say a word."

"Oh, I know you won't," he laughed until he began coughing.

"You're crazy!" she yelled. "You're fucking crazy. You won't get away with this."

Officer Bradley walked over to where Claire sat with her back against the tree. He kneeled in front of her and runs the back of his right hand against her face. His touch and the smell of his cologne made her cringe.

He reached into his back pocket and pulled out a long-handled knife.

He then took the tip of the blade, slowly ran it from her throat, then down between her breast. He stopped and gently pressed in, causing Claire to take a deep breath.

"Don't worry darling I'm not going to kill you," he said with a grin. "At least not just yet. Let's have a little fun first."

She felt a little prick as he then took his knife and dragged it down a little more, cutting open Claire's gown.

"You don't have to do this," she begged, but he wasn't listening. "I won't say a word if you let me go. I will pack my things and leave town. Please, you're better than this."

Officer Bradley stared at Claire and

smiled. She didn't know if it was a good smile or bad, but she prayed that it was good. "Hold up your hands," he said, and she did as she was told.

"What are you going to do?" she asked.

Officer Bradley said nothing. He took hold of her hands and cut her hands free, followed by her feet. He nodded his head, letting her know to leave. Claire's heart skipped with joy.

"Thank you," she said with glee, but something didn't feel right. She hesitated at first, but suddenly she made her move. Her leg was still hurting from the gunshot earlier. She was in no mood to run, but she needed to move as fast as she could. She began to walk away but was stopped when she heard him loading his gun. She slowly turned around to Officer Bradley pointing his gun at her.

"Did you think I was going to let you just walk away?" he said.

Claire couldn't say a word. She only stood there thinking this could be it. She closed her eyes and began thinking of her daughter who could be in danger. When she opened her eyes she instantly felt relieved.

"Drop the weapon!" Detective Armstrong yelled out as he came in sight. He kept his gun pointed at Officer Bradley while he made his way towards Claire. "I said drop your weapon!" he yells again.

Officer Bradley dropped his weapon and held his hands up in front of him.

"Now kick your weapon towards me," Daniel said as he watched Officer Bradley do as he was told. With his gun still pointing at him, he reached down and grabbed the gun. "Here take this," he said as he handed the gun to Claire.

"What am I supposed to do with this? She asked.

"Use it if needed," said Detective Armstrong.

"Ok," she said nervously. Claire had never used a gun before, but today would be her first.

Detective Armstrong walked towards Officer Bradley, but immediately stopped when he saw a woman coming walking towards them.

"What's wrong detective? Changed your

mind?" Officer Bradley asked with a sly grin on his face. A grin that soon changed when he turned around and saw disturbed Peggy walking towards them.

Claire made her way closer and stood behind Detective Armstrong. "It's Peggy Woolrich," she stated. "She stays near. Let me talk to her."

"No, stay back. Something doesn't feel right. Something is wrong with her," he said as he pushed Claire further behind him.

"There's nothing wrong with her. She's going through a lot you know. Maybe she's scared or looking for help,"

said Claire as she made her way from around Detective Armstrong.

"Where are you going?" Detective Armstrong asked as he quickly grabbed Claire's arm.

"I'm going to see what's wrong," she said as she snatched her arm away and began walking towards Peggy. Her walk slowed as she noticed the look in Peggy's eyes.

Something was seriously wrong. The

look in Peggy's eyes were of something she has never seen before. They were dark and cold, while her body seemed pale and lifeless.

Claire's eyes wandered down to Peggy's right hand. Even with the overgrown trees, weeds and vines, it was no match in hiding the bloody ax that she was holding in her hand. She knew then, this wasn't the same Peggy that she had just visited a day ago. She could hear Detective Armstrong calling her name. She began walking backwards until she bumped into Detective Armstrong, who now had his gun aimed at Peggy as she came closer.

"Shoot her," Officer Bradley called out as they all began walking backwards. He wanted her dead too, because he feared that she could ruin his name and his career.

The closer she came, they all could see how fragile her body looked as she dragged her ax against the ground. Blood splatter covered her dress as she began to lift her ax. Officer Bradley didn't waste any time as he reached into the waistband of the back of his pants and pulled out a second gun and points it at Peggy.

"Fucking shoot her!" he yells. "Shoot her now or I will!" he yells again.

Detective Armstrong stood there terrified of what he was seeing. Shit like this only happens in movies. They didn't happen in real life.

Claire looked over and was surprised to see Officer Bradley holding a gun. "No you can't shoot!" she yells right as Officer Bradley fired his gun but was too late.

"You killed me," said Peggy in a croaky voice, but she was no longer Peggy. She then swung her ax, slicing Officer Bradley's throat.

He clutched his throat with his left hand, as the blood seeped through his fingers. Still holding his gun in his right hand, he aims at her as his world started to become blurry. He then fired one last shot, striking Peggy in the right shoulder, hoping to slow her down, but it didn't work.

"You will die just like the others," she said as she lifted her ax, then swung it, striking Officer Bradley again. This time with so much force, that his head was dismembered from his body, before falling onto the ground.

"Oh my God," Claire said as she looked at Officer Bradley's lifeless body on the ground.

Peggy turned and looked at Claire with evil in her eyes. Detective Armstrong wasn't taking a chance...not tonight. He then pointed his gun at Peggy and fired a shot, striking her in the same right shoulder, but that still didn't stop her from coming.

"Daniel what are you doing? Please don't kill her," Claire begged."

"I don't want to kill her, but it's either us or her," he stated before firing another shot. This time striking her in the left leg.

"What are you doing? You're going to kill her!" Claire screamed.

"She's not Peggy. She will kill you," he said as he fired another shot to the abdomen.

She kept coming, nothing was working. Detective Armstrong and Claire just looked at each other. They were out of ideas. Then suddenly they hear a young girls voice coming from Peggy.

"Please don't kill my mother," she

cried. Then suddenly her cry faded, and she began laughing hysterically in a guttural voice. "You can't kill me you fool, I'm already dead," she laughed as she took her hand and grabbed Detective Armstrong around his neck. With powerful force, she throws him aside hitting a tree. She continued to slowly walk towards Claire.

"Sarah, I know you're in there, don't do this," Claire begged. "Think about your mom. If you do this, you will be as guilty as the ones that killed you," she cried. "I know what they did to you."

Peggy wasn't listening. Sarah had control and the only thing that was on her mind was revenge by death.

"Sarah please don't do this. Think of your friends," said Claire.

"I have no friends," she said as she lifted her ax in the air.

"No!" Detective Armstrong yelled as he crawled to his gun and fired a shot, hitting Peggy in the back.

Peggy gasped for air, "You cannot kill what you cannot see," she said before falling to the ground.

Claire rushed to Detective Armstrong's side. "Are you ok?" she asked.

"Yeah. Will probably be a little sore in the morning," he said. "But I'm ok."

"Thank you for saving me," she said with a smile.

"Don't thank me yet. This is just the beginning," he said with fear and concern in his voice as they both looked at Peggy's body on the ground.

"She's alive," Claire said as she hurried to Peggy. "Peggy, hold on we're going to get help," she said as she took hold of Peggy's hand. "It's going to be ok."

"Your daughter…she's in trouble," she cried. "I'm sorry."

"It's not your fault," said Claire.

"I just wanted my daughter back. I didn't mean for this to happen," she whispered.

"You didn't mean for what to happen?" Claire asked curiously. "Peggy… don't you dare go. Wake up… please," she cried, before giving up.

Peggy tried to keep her eyes open, but the pain physically and emotionally was too much to bare. Finally she gave in to the darkness. Claire looked up at Detective Armstrong with tears in her eyes.

"You can't save everyone Claire," he said.

"We need to leave now. My daughter could be in danger." she said. "I can't lose her."

Detective Armstrong helped Claire off the ground. "Let's go," he said as he looked down at his watch. It was getting late and he wanted to get out of the woods before it got dark.

CHAPTER TWENTY

Detective Armstrong and Claire made their way to Claire's house. Only to find it engulfed in flames. They both hurried out of the car, as Claire headed for the front door.

"What are you doing?" Detective Armstrong asked.

"I'm going to save my daughter," she replied.

"You're hurt, you won't make it out," he stated.

"I have to get my daughter out. She's all that I have," Claire said with great determination.

"You could die," said Detective Armstrong.

"Well, I will die trying," she said before heading off again to the door.

"Wait!" he yelled. Claire stopped to look back at him. "I will go inside, while you check the back."

Claire just stood there staring at Detective Armstrong as if he didn't understand her plan.

"Look, I promise I will come back with her. You have my word. My word is everything to me. Just trust me," he stated.

"Ok. I trust you. Don't come back without her," she said while on the verge of tears. "I will go check the back."

"Ok," he replied.

Claire made her way to the back of the house and began calling Jess's name, but there was no answer. She could see the smoke coming from out of the windows and began to panic. She said she would only check the back of the house, but couldn't resist the urge to go in.

"Jess," she calls again, but no answer. She looked at the door and realized the handle was missing and a key was broken off inside of the lock. She thought of maybe trying to break the door in, but she knew she wasn't strong enough. She needed to think of another way to get in. "Jess!" she yelled out as loud as she could until she heard a knocking. "Jess! Jess is that you?!"

"Mom!" Jess yelled.

"Where are you?" Claire asked.

"Mom I'm down here. Mom help me!"

"I'm trying to find you," Claire replied. "Just keep talking so I can find you." Claire could hear Jess coughing. The fire was getting out of control.

"Mom!"

"I'm coming," Claire said as she began removing the vines that covered a wooden door located near the ground, leading to the basement. "Jess it's locked. There's a chain on it. I can't open it. Just hold on ok."

At that moment Claire could hear Detective Armstrong's voice through the wooden door. She felt a sense of relief that she's been waiting on for the longest.

"Daniel the door has a chain on it. I can't open it," Claire called out.

"Stand back from the door," he replied.

Claire did as she was told and within seconds Detective Armstrong fired two rounds, shooting off the lock. The longest seconds ever, seemed like hours. Claire waited and finally the doors flew open. The sight of seeing her daughter was the best feeling ever. Today was only one day, but it felt like eternity.

"Mom!" Jess yelled with tears in her eyes as she ran to her mom and hugged her.

"Jess! Are you ok?" she cried as she held her daughter tight in her arms.

"I'm ok," Jess replied.

Claire looked at Detective Armstrong, "thank you," she said.

He only smiled in return. He didn't have children of his own but could only imagine what Claire was going through.

"Where are your friends? I thought they were with you," Claire asked her daughter.

"They left me mom. After finding this secret room in the basement with my name written all over the walls in blood, they said I was the one she wanted," said Jess. "Friends. I sure can pick them."

"It's not your fault. I guess your old

friends weren't too bad after all," she said with a smile. "Here, let me take this." Claire took the necklace Jess was wearing from around her neck.

Jess stared at the necklace as her mom removed it. So much had happened that she had forgot that she was wearing it. She didn't bother to argue with her mom. She knew the reason why she shouldn't wear it. It belongs to Sarah.

"You don't need this. I will get you another one," said Claire.

"We need to get going. We can wait in the front for the emergency crew to arrive," Detective Armstrong said as they began making their way towards the front.

Just as they walked passed the wooden doors, Claire threw the necklace down into the basement. It was her way of saying goodbye to the past.

She cradled her daughter as they sat on the ground by Detective Armstrong's car, waiting for the ambulance to arrive. Soon blue lights and sirens from the police cars filled the air, along with the ambulance and fire truck. Claire and Jess sat there watching as the flames and smoke began pouring out of their house.

"Are you sure you're ok Jess?" Claire asked.

"I'm fine mom. What about you?" asked Jess.

"I'm good. Just a little sore, but I will make it," she said with a smile.

Jess smiled back. "Mom, I know how much you love it here, but I don't want to stay here."

"Jess if you want to leave...we will leave, but first I need you to go back with your dad while I'm in the hospital recovering," Claire suggested.

"Mom, why? I don't want to go without you" said Jess.

"Because it's what's best for the both of you right now," said a male voice.

Claire and Jess looked around and saw Frank standing behind them. Claire's soon to be ex-husband was staring down at them.

"Dad?"

"Frank? What are you doing here? I

called you days ago," Claire said as her and Jess both stood up. She tried her best not to show her anger.

"What are you talking about. I just got back into town last night," said Frank.

"So, your phone doesn't work out of town?"

"Claire what are you talking about? I never got any text or call from you until this morning?"

"I know when I called you. I even texted you right after."

"Mom," Jess said as she tried interrupting the conversation between her two parents.

Claire and Frank continued arguing like usual. Nothing seemed to have changed between the two of them. Claire knew that she still had feelings for Frank. She also knew that being apart was probably for the best.

Their conversation ended as she heard someone calling Jess's name. She looked around and saw Jess running towards the burning house.

"Jess what are you doing!" Claire screamed. She wanted to run after her but was held back by Frank.

"You can't go in there Claire! The flames are out of control! Frank said.

"There's someone in there!" Jess yelled as she pointed up towards her room. The house was engulfed in flames as she disappeared into the burning house.

"Jess no!" her mother screamed. The tears flooded her eyes as Detective Armstrong, who stood from afar came over to reassure her everything will be ok.

"The Chief has some guys inside now searching for Jess," he stated. "Can't promise anything, but I'm sure they will give it their all."

Claire couldn't say or do anything. She only nodded as she stared up at their burning house before focusing on Jess's bedroom window. She breaks away from Franks grip and walks as close as she could towards the burning house. Through the smoke she could see someone standing there. A girl, smiling down at her before disappearing.

Within minutes, which seemed like hours, the firefighters came running out with Jess. She was still alive. Claire rushed to her daughter with such relief.

"Jess are you ok?" Claire asked but Jess said nothing.

"We need to get her to the hospital to make sure she's ok," the firefighter stated.

"Ok, but I'm going with her," Claire said as she climbed into the ambulance by Jess's side.

THREE DAYS LATER

The nurse pushed Jess in the wheelchair as Claire walked beside them. She insisted on walking, but her only concern was Jess. That night when they arrived at the hospital. Jess became lethargic and was saying weird things in her sleep. The doctors ran tests and later gave her a clean bill of health. She was fine...her baby was fine. The doctors assured her it was just the medicine, but other than that, she had nothing to worry about.

They arrived at the patient pickup area just as Jess's dad showed up.

"Right on time finally," Claire said out loud. Frank is never on time for anything. She was just glad that he showed up.

Frank placed his car in park as he got out. He walked over to where they all stood. "Claire," he said as he gave a quick smile.

The nurse rolled the wheelchair closer to the car. She held the back of the wheelchair as Frank helped his daughter into the car.

"Thank you," Claire said to the nurse.

"You're welcome. Get some rest," the nurse replied before walking away.

Claire had been up all-night, and it showed on her face. She had been checking on Jess, when she should have been resting herself.

"I will," she said with a friendly smile. She turned to Jess as she bent down and gave her a kiss upon her forehead. "I will see you soon, ok."

Jess didn't say a word. She just continued looking straight ahead but Claire knew she would be back to the old Jess once she left this town.

"I love you Jess," she said as she hugged her and held her in her embrace. She didn't want to leave her, but she knew it was for the best. She closed the door and waited for the car to pull off.

Her phone began ringing. She looked down to see Detective Armstrong calling her. "Hello," she answered.

"Claire, I hope you don't mind me

calling you on your work cell. I didn't know any other way to reach you," he said.

"No it's fine. Is everything ok?" she asked as she watched the car slowly begin to drive away.

"We're over at Peggy Woolrich's house and you're not going to believe this," he said as he began to explain the situation.

Claire couldn't believe what she was hearing. She looked up to see Jess now staring at her, smiling through the window while holding the same necklace she tossed into the burning house.

"No!" she yelled as she tried to stop the car, but it was too late. They were already gone. "I have to go," she said as she ended the call with Detective Armstrong and began dialing Frank.

ONE HOUR LATER

The ride was quiet most of the way. The only thing you could hear was the music playing and Frank's voice on the phone. He was always on the phone. Always too busy for family. He would always say that he was paving a brighter future for his family, which is why he spent long hours at the office. That may be true, but they will never know. At least, not in this lifetime.

"Why is your mother calling me? Call your mother and see what she wants," he said to Jess.

Jess sat there as if she didn't hear him talking. She stared straight ahead, showing no expressions at all. Her face was emotionless.

"Hey, you hear me? I said call your mother," he said again. "Jess."

"My name isn't Jess," she replied.

"What? What are you talking about? I named you myself. I know what your name is," he said as he placed his phone down.

"My name isn't Jess," she said in an alarming and eerie voice, followed by a creepy laugh. "You thought you could get away."

Suddenly the music faded and the conversation between Frank and Officer Bradley filled the air.

Frank looked over at Jess. Sweat began to form across his face. She was right, she wasn't Jess. Her eyes were all black and blood ran from them.

Right as Frank reached for his phone, Jess grabbed his hand and began bending it all the way back, breaking it in two. He screamed from the excruciating pain as he tried to focus on the road and Jess.

"I'm sorry! Ok I'm sorry!" he cried hysterically. He apologized over and over, but his time was now up.

She reached under her seat and pulled out her ax. Frank looked over at her with wide eyes, screaming from the top of his lungs for what was about to happen next. The car came to a complete stop. The only thing you could see from the outside of the car, were blood splattered windows as she exited the car and walked away.